Lucy Maud and Me

Lucy Maud and Me

a novel by

Mary Frances Coady

An imprint of
Beach Holme Publishing
Vancouver, B.C.

This book is published by Beach Holme Publishing, #226—2040 West
12th Ave., Vancouver, BC, V6J 2G2. This is a Sandcastle Book.
Teacher's guide available from Beach Holme Publishing, call toll-free
1-888-551-6655.

The publisher and author acknowledge
the generous assistance of The Canada
Council and the BC Ministry of Small
Business, Tourism and Culture.

THE CANADA COUNCIL | LE CONSEIL DES ARTS
FOR THE ARTS | DU CANADA
SINCE 1957 | DEPUIS 1957

The text of this book was inspired by the writings of L.M. Montgomery,
including *The Selected Journals of L.M. Montgomery, volumes I - IV*,
Oxford University Press, 1985, 1987, 1992, 1998.

Editor: Joy Gugeler
Cover Illustration: Janet Wilson
Production and Design: Teresa Bubela
Printed in Canada

Canadian Cataloguing in Publication Data

Coady, Mary Frances.
  Lucy Maud and me

  (A Sandcastle Book.)
  ISBN 0-88878-398-1

  1. Montgomery, L. M. (Lucy Maud), 1874-1942–Juvenile fiction. I.
Title.
PS8555.O232L82 1999   jC813'.54   C99-910310-5
PZ7.C6278Lu 1999

For the Holubowich family and especially
for Stefania

Chapter One

A man's voice echoed just above Laura's head. She half-opened her eyes and then closed them again, clinging to the jumbled faces in her dream. She stretched her legs and rubbed the stiff spots in her shoulder and arm. As she did, her book slid off her lap and onto the floor. Beneath her feet, the wheels of the train slowed to a rumble.

The train conductor smiled down at her, his pink cheeks shining. "Just about there," he said. He stooped, picked up the book and handed it back to her.

Laura blinked and looked out the window. The last time she had looked out, she'd seen mile after mile of trees, broken only by the occasional lakeshore and rough beach. Now she saw street after street of houses, red brick and strung together in lines. The train must be entering Toronto.

What had happened to the people in her dream—her father in his air force uniform, her mother's tear-stained face? Where were Jennifer and Wendy? They had seemed so close, playing hopscotch on the dirt road and giggling. And Peter?

Loneliness welled up inside her; it was as if everyone familiar to her had suddenly disappeared. She considered asking the conductor if she might stay on the train until it headed north to Rocky Falls again. But the spring flood warnings had begun and the whole town had been put on evacuation notice. Her father was gone for now; he had enlisted in the Royal Canadian Air Force over a year ago. A call had gone out for surgeons and he had answered. Now that he was working in a military hospital in England, thousands of miles away, he wasn't even able to come home on leave. Her mother was still working full time in a munitions factory and in the evening often helped package up parcels for Canadian soldiers. She intended to continue unless she was forced out by the flood. Because her mother would be working both day and night, she had insisted Laura visit her grandfather while school was out, rather than risk her staying home alone.

She'd never been away from home before, and although it was exciting to be travelling three hours by train to a big city, she felt afraid. What if she got lost? How would she get along without her mother?

"But I can look after myself here, at home," she had pleaded. "I don't have to go anywhere. Or—I know—we can go to Toronto together. Or maybe Grandpa can come here." She stopped, reluctant to admit what was coming next, but then blurted it out. "I just don't want to go by myself!"

No amount of arguing had changed her mother's mind. Staring out as the train passed block after block of unfamiliar houses, she wished her mother had relented and come too. She looked down at the book in her lap, *The Story Girl*. On the cover was the picture of a young girl looking toward a field of daisies. In the distance stood an orchard. The girl's hair flowed onto her shoulders and she was sitting with her head thrown back, smiling, carefree. Laura picked up the book and leafed through the pages. She had lost her place. She remembered now what the book was about: a group of young people were spending a golden summer together on Prince Edward Island. Sara was the Story Girl, fourteen years of age, who told spell-binding stories about the old folk in the village and their long-dead relatives. The others gathered around her whenever she spoke, caught up in her web of magic.

Prince Edward Island. That was where Grandpa had come from. She stretched and smiled, for the moment forgetting her gloomy mood. She'd soon be seeing him again. For as long as she could remember, he'd come up to Rocky Falls to spend the month of July with her and her parents. "Ah, the fresh air of the country," he always said, taking in deep breaths as he stood in their back yard. "The city's no place to spend the summer," he grumbled. "Especially Toronto. It's hot as Hades this time of year."

He spent day after day, sitting and talking on the front verandah. Often in the evenings, Laura sat on the top step while her father worked in the garden and her mother knitted. The knitting needles clicked in rhythm with Grandpa's voice as he told tales of his childhood on the Island. She loved hearing him tell of how he walked miles over frozen fields to a one-room school and dried his mittens on the black pot-bellied stove under the picture of Queen Victoria, which hung on the wall beside the Union Jack.

"We looked at that picture every morning, the Queen with her white veil and grumpy-looking face, and by jeepers if we didn't settle down after singing 'God Save the Queen'. We were afraid she'd reach down from the wall and clip us one if we didn't behave." He told her about the slates they'd used instead of notebooks, and about the chestnut tree not far from the school where older girls and boys sometimes carved their initials. He had left as a young man to work in the harvest on the prairies before becoming a doctor in Toronto, but his heart remained in the Prince Edward Island of his boyhood.

Laura smiled to herself. It would be nice to see Grandpa again.

The chugging of the train engine had slowed, and the wheels were moving at a crawl. From the windows across the aisle, Lake Ontario stretched clear to the horizon. Then the train passed into an enclosed area, with steel rafters rising up to a high dome, gave a final shudder, and jerked to a stop. The door at the end of the railway car opened and once again the conductor appeared.

"Union Station, Toronto," he called out. "End of the line. Everyone out here."

All around her, passengers rose from their seats and pulled boxes and suitcases from overhead racks. Laura picked up her book and placed it in her knapsack. The conductor stopped beside her, reached up and pulled down a small brown suitcase. "There you are, miss," he said. "Enjoy your stay in Toronto. Is someone meeting you?"

"My grandfather," said Laura in a small voice, wondering for a second if indeed Grandpa would be there to meet her.

The conductor helped her down the steps, and then she was swept up with the stream of passengers making their way down a flight of stairs. They climbed up another flight into an enormous lobby where hundreds of people were milling about. Men in uniform—soldiers with khaki sacks thrown over their shoulders, air force men like her father in their blue-grey suits, and even sailors in their white caps and bell-bottom trousers—were everywhere, laughing, walking with their arms around young women who wore long faces and looked close to tears.

"Laura, over here!" she heard from somewhere amid the sea of faces. She looked around. There was Grandpa coming toward her wearing a blue wool sweater and the black cap he always wore to cover his thinning hair. His eyebrows and moustache were as bushy as ever, but a bit whiter than she'd remembered from last summer. She ran with clumsy steps toward him holding her suitcase in one hand and her knapsack in the other. "Grandpa!"

He stooped down to kiss her on the cheek. The roughness of his moustache and the faint smell of liniment he used for sore muscles was comforting. He took her suitcase and looked Laura up and down, as if inspecting her. Familiar crinkles formed around his eyes.

"Well, well," he said. "My only granddaughter is growing up so quickly I can hardly keep up with her. Let me see now, where do you come up to? Stand up to my shoulder here." He stood at attention, and she stood next to him. He craned his neck, peering down at her. "You haven't reached my shoulder yet, but you're well above my elbow. That's—what—about four or five inches since last summer?"

Laura grinned and nodded. He picked up her suitcase again and took her by the arm. "Let's get ourselves out of here. Ever since the war started, this station has been a madhouse with the enlisted men coming through from all over. Because of all the training camps around southern Ontario, they're talking about reducing train services to civilians even more than they've done already." He smiled down at her. "But thank heavens that hasn't happened yet, and you've been able to visit me."

Grandpa's hand was steady and firm on her arm. Looking down at his big feet padding next to hers, she noticed white and brown dog hairs on the cuffs of his trousers.

"Do you still have Sam, Grandpa?"

"I sure do. You'll see him as soon as we get you back to the house."

Outside on the street, Laura was amazed at the height of the buildings and the bustle of the street. A man in a maroon uniform stood outside the brass doors of the Royal York Hotel. Car after car passed in front of them in a haze of fumes. Horns honked. A milk wagon drawn by a heavy dray horse drove by, the clip-clop sound blending strangely with honking car horns. A group of soldiers lounged, whistling and laughing loudly, on large piles of baggage, their brown caps set back on their heads.

"We're lucky to still have taxis," Grandpa said, leading Laura toward a line of red and yellow cabs. "Now that we have the new gasoline rationing law, who knows how much longer they'll be able to stay in business?"

It was a relief to be in the safety of a taxi. There were so many people and cars and traffic noise! She thought longingly of the quiet streets of Rocky Falls, where friendly people always said hello and cars stopped if you wanted to cross the road. And just beyond the streets were the country roads that beckoned. She and Peter biked for hours there last summer.

"How is your mother?" Grandpa asked gently as the taxi turned onto Lakeshore Boulevard.

"Fine," said Laura, not knowing what else to say. She looked outside instead, at the lake.

There was silence for a moment and then he said, his voice quiet, "Any news from your dad?"

For the first time since she had arrived, Laura felt a catch in her throat. "I got a letter from him," she said, her voice shaky. She pressed her fingers into the palm of her hand. She didn't want to cry in front of her grandfather. "On thin blue paper. He folded it so that it made its own envelope. He's in London. That's where the King and Queen and the princesses live. He didn't say if he's seen them yet."

"What *did* he say then?"

"He said the food is pretty boring. They just have dried mutton and Brussels sprouts to eat. He said he wished he could have a hot dog sometimes, and some of Mom's chocolate cake. And he said people use funny words like 'lorry' instead of 'truck', and 'cinema' instead of 'movie theatre'." She swallowed and looked down at the knapsack on her lap.

Grandpa pulled at his sweater sleeve and looked over at her with a twinkle in his eye. "And if you called this a 'sweater' over in England, people would laugh at you."

"Why?" asked Laura.

"They'd say, 'That's not a sweater. It's a cardigan. And do you know what they call pullover sweaters? They call them jumpers."

"Jumpers?! How do you know that, Grandpa"

"Why, didn't you know? I was over there during the last war. The 'Great War' we called it. I suppose if we're going to call the war that's going on now the Second World War, we'll have to call that one the First World War."

Laura's mouth hung open. By now she had forgotten her

sadness. "Were you in the same place as my dad is?" she asked eagerly.

"No, I was in the army, not the air force. I was stationed in a field hospital in the south of England, where they brought some of the wounded lads across the English Channel."

"Did you see soldiers fighting?"

"No, I just saw the evidence of the fighting. Men in pretty bad shape. But your dad now, in London—one never knows when the Blitz will start up again—"

Laura felt Grandpa shift beside her. She looked over at him. His mouth was open, as if he was about to say more, then he closed it and sighed. After another moment, he asked, "How's school?"

"Fine," she said. "I got a hundred percent in spelling last week. We have a girls' softball team now. I'm pretty good at pitching."

"That's my granddaughter," he laughed, "a scholar and a sportswoman—oh, and speaking of pitching, look here." He pointed out the window to a large stadium set against the lake. "That's the Sunnyside Stadium. The Sunnyside Ladies' softball team plays there. They play a fine game of softball. Crowds come from all over to watch them." He smiled down at her. "Maybe you'll be one of the Sunnyside Ladies some day."

Before Laura had a chance to answer, he went on, "And look up ahead." A collection of huge buildings with domes and arches and towers were clustered together, like a group of castles. "See, there are the gates of the C.N.E. just ahead."

"What does C.N.E. stand for?" asked Laura.

"It's the Canadian National Exhibition, the biggest exhibition in Canada," Grandpa explained. "People come here from all over the country." They both turned their heads as the cab sped past the great arched gates. "It's too bad you won't be here in August to see the exhibition and go on the midway rides. On the other hand, it may not be operating this year. I heard on the news that the Ex may be closed down soon so the buildings can be used for armed forces training. But look over here, that's Sunnyside Park. It's a terrific beach and amusement park. Things don't get into full swing until Victoria Day, so it's about a month early yet."

Looking out the window, Laura saw roller coasters and ferris wheels and other midway rides standing still along the shore and the colourful fronts of concession stands boarded up. Beyond them stood tall life-guard chairs on an empty beach and, in a gazebo, a family seemed to be setting up an early-spring picnic. Gulls swooped back and forth.

A hard knot had formed inside her stomach. Why had Grandpa sighed and stopped talking about her father? Her mom had said that her dad was in England, nowhere near the war. He wasn't supposed to be in any danger. Was her mother wrong? The Blitz that Grandpa had begun talking about—where had she heard that word before? Then she remembered, and the knot inside hardened. Soon after the war started, some of the women in Rocky Falls saved up bits of material and got together to make quilts for people in the air-raid shelters. It was because of the Blitz, her mother had said, explaining that Nazi war planes dropped bombs over the English cities at night. Was her father then—?

The taxi made a turn and now the lake was behind them. "We're getting close to home now," said Grandpa. "This is Swansea. Used to be a village, but it's pretty much a part of

Toronto now."

"Are there any kids in your neighbourhood, Grandpa?" asked Laura.

"Kids? Well, not really. Let's see, who's in the neighbour-hood? Now that I think of it, I'm afraid it's not a very exciting lot."

The taxi began to wind up a steep hill, past thick bushes and trees, and for a moment it seemed to Laura that they were out in the country.

"That's the Humber River, down there below all those bushes," said Grandpa, pointing.

At the top of the hill, houses appeared on both sides of the road. "Here we have the Hastings," said Grandpa, pointing to the one on the left. "They're a family that's very private. And over there are the Norberts. Their kids are grown and off to school. Right across the street is the Macdonalds' place. The Reverend Ewan Macdonald, a retired Presbyterian minister. Poor man."

Laura felt dejected. What was she going to do here with no one but old people and retired ministers?

"Why is he a poor man?" she asked.

"I'll explain later. What's more interesting is that his wife is—" But before he could finish, the cab came to a stop in front of a white house shaded by oak and maple trees.

Chapter Two

Opening the car door, Laura noticed there were tiny green shoots on the trees, unlike in Rocky Falls where the trees were still bare even though it was past the middle of April.

"Let's see if Sam is around," said Grandpa, breaking into her thoughts as he came around the side of the taxi, Laura's suitcase in his hand. He opened the gate. "Aha! Here's the official welcome."

A brown and white spaniel bounded toward them, his big ears flapping. Laura put down her knapsack to stroke him as he jumped up at her.

Inside the front door of the house, she stopped and looked around. The house seemed larger and more grand than their house in Rocky Falls. One wall was lined with bookcases. In the living room, which was furnished with brocade sofas and soft white lamps, she spotted a familiar photograph on the mantel-piece. She and her mother were sitting side by side, smiling into the camera. Laura was dressed in her best blouse and skirt. Long braids hung down over her shoulders, with two big bows. Her mother had had the photograph taken for her father and had sent it to Grandpa as well. Laura hated the picture. She had wanted to wear her hair down, to look more grown-up. But her mother had been firm, saying, "I want your father to see you as you are now."

"My two favourite ladies in all the world," said Grandpa as Laura gazed at the photograph. "Now come, I want you to meet Bobbie, my housekeeper."

At the back of the house, the kitchen was bright with gleaming linoleum on the floor, the walls lined with clean white cupboards. Standing at the stove was a slim, pretty woman, about the same age as Laura's new teacher, who had come to Rocky Falls straight out of Teachers' College. She wore bright red lipstick, and her curly brown hair was tied back with a yellow bow. She wore a white housedress splashed with brightly coloured flowers.

"Bobbie, this is the long-awaited Laura," said Grandpa. He turned to Laura and said, "Bobbie does the cooking and housecleaning for me. She has supper ready for us and will soon be going home for the day. But first, she'll show you your room."

Bobbie wiped her hands on a towel and came toward Laura. "Well, it is lovely to meet you. Here, give me your knapsack." Her smile was warm, and she smelled of perfume.

Upstairs, Laura gasped with surprise as Bobbie opened the door to her bedroom. The room was filled with white wicker furniture. On the bed was a bedspread patterned with pink roses and festooned with pillows. Best of all was the window across from the bed. White muslin curtains covered the window and in front was a window seat, just like Laura had seen in movies. She ran to the window seat, knelt on the padded cushion, and pulled aside the curtains to look out.

Beyond their trees, on the other side of the street, Laura could see a house with timbered beams. The dark wooden front door gave the house an impenetrable look. It made her think of Grimms' fairy tales and gingerbread houses. Laura shuddered but remained kneeling on the window seat and gazed at the house. Who did Grandpa say lived there?

"Let's get you unpacked," Bobbie said, and Laura turned back to the room. Bobbie set down an armful of towels and smoothed out the bedspread. She lifted Laura's suitcase and set it on the bed. "May I take your things out?" Laura nodded, and Bobbie began putting her clothes on hangers. Laura noticed a small diamond ring on her left hand.

"What a shame for you, you poor dear, that there's no one your age here," said Bobbie. I was saying to your grandfather the other day that you might be bored in this neighbourhood. He'll not be much company, having to be at his office all day. His medical practice is much too big for a doctor in his late sixties, if you ask me. Patients are always hounding him for one thing or another. I hope you won't get lost in the shuffle. Goodness knows, you won't find much entertainment in me. I just go around all day cooking and cleaning and minding my own business." She gave Laura a mournful look. "Even the old folk aren't all that friendly in this part of the city if you ask me—your grandfather excepted, of course," Bobbie went on. "He's a gentleman if there ever was one. Do you have things to keep yourself amused?"

Laura opened her knapsack. "I've got a book to read," she said, "and maybe Grandpa can take me to the library."

"Maybe so," said Bobbie. "Come to think of it..." She put her hand to her mouth. "No, no, why would I even think of suggesting it? It's none of my business." She opened a bureau drawer, a pile of clothes in her hand.

"What?" asked Laura.

"Well, not being much of a reader myself, I really wouldn't know," said Bobbie, folding Laura's things and placing them in the drawer. "But Mrs. Macdonald across the street—the poor old Reverend's wife—they say she writes books. If you like to read—but no, as I say, it's not my affair. She's awfully cranky, anyway." She closed Laura's suitcase. "But who wouldn't be, looking after that man all day and all night?"

Laura pulled *The Story Girl* from her knapsack and began to leaf through it, trying to find the place where she had left off reading it on the train. She was now only half-listening.

"Well, I really don't know," Bobbie continued. "But the poor woman is a real case. I'd avoid her."

"Who's a case, Bobbie?" Grandpa asked, at the door.

"Mrs. Macdonald. Oh, I know you have a soft spot for her, Dr. Campbell, but she seems a strange one to me. I can't figure her out."

"Maud Macdonald? Well now, I knew her as a girl. She wasn't always like she is now. She was—but look at that!"

Laura looked up to see her grandfather pointing to the book in her hands.

"I'll be!" he exclaimed. "That's one of her books, one of Maud's books! Look at the name of the author. 'L.M. Montgomery.' That's Maud Macdonald!"

Laura looked at the book, confused. Grandpa went on: "Lucy Maud. Montgomery was her name before she was married. She's the pride of Cavendish."

"What do you mean, Grandpa? Where's Cavendish?"

"Why, that's where I lived for a short while, back in Prince Edward Island."

"And?"

"And little Maud was one of the girls in the school there. Funny little thing was Maud. Talked to herself a lot. They said she believed in fairies and such creatures. A fine lass all the same. High-spirited and jolly. And very clever."

Laura looked down at the book again, at the cover picture of the girl who seemed to be gazing into the distance. She couldn't believe it!

"I read another book by her," she said. "It was called *Anne of Green Gables*. The librarian told me if I liked that book, I'd like this one too. And I do."

"A great shame," Grandpa continued. He shook his head. "She's had it hard these past years. She seems to have turned in on herself now. Of course, one can hardly blame her." He looked at his watch. "Bobbie, it's past the time you usually leave. As for Laura and me—it's suppertime."

✧

At supper in the panelled dining room, Laura continued to question her grandfather about Mrs. Macdonald. "Are you *sure* she's the same person as L.M. Montgomery, Grandpa? Did you know her when she was my age? What was she like?"

Grandpa laughed as he scooped up a forkful of potatoes. "In many ways she was just a normal youngster like the rest of us," he said. "In the summertime we picked berries and went trout-fishing and walked for miles in the sand along the shoreline. In the winter we sledded down the hills and went to parties in each other's homes. Maud was often the life of the party."

"Grandpa, is she, is she a nice lady? Do you think she'll she talk to me?"

"Who? Maud?" Her grandfather laughed again. "Well now, 'nice' may not be the best word to describe her. She doesn't bother the neighbors much, I'll give her that. She keeps to herself. Soon after we moved in here and I discovered that it was Maud living across the street, I went over and introduced myself to the two of them, thinking to get re-acquainted after all these years. The husband was cordial enough, though quiet. Maud seemed to remember me, but didn't want to reminisce about the old days. She seemed distracted, as if she had too much on her mind. She's not been well lately. It's her nerves, mainly. At least, that's my understanding."

"What do you mean?" asked Lucy.

"Well, she seems to get easily upset. She's nervous and anxious about small things that you or I wouldn't bother ourselves with."

"What kinds of things?"

Grandpa wiped his plate with a piece of bread. He chewed a moment in silence. "Oh, I don't know. It's a big chore just to get herself through the day, I imagine. Of course, it isn't any wonder, with him the way he is."

"What's wrong with him?" she asked.

"You ask a lot of questions that aren't easy to answer, young lady," he said, smiling at her. "I've never been told, but it may be a condition called senile dementia. Do you know what that means?"

Laura shook her head.

"Sometimes when people get old, they—well, their minds

start to go. Just like your body sometimes begins to wear out—your joints get stiff, and your eyes aren't as good as they used to be, and your hearing begins to go—well, it's sometimes the same with the mind. You imagine things that aren't true, you begin to think your friends are against you. Anyway, enough of all that. Here, let me take your plate and I'll get us some dessert."

Grandpa piled her plate on top of his and rose from the table. "Having a wife who's famous doesn't help either," he continued. "Times are changing. Women like your mother are working in factories and enlisting in the armed services. But the way we, Ewan and I, were brought up—why, it was considered a man's duty to support his wife. Ewan's wife is supporting *him*."

He disappeared through the swinging door into the kitchen and re-emerged with two dishes of canned fruit. "A special treat to welcome you," he said, setting one of the dishes in front of Laura and the other in front of himself. "I don't know if you've noticed, but anything in tins is almost impossible to get anymore. Every bit of tin and steel is being used for the war effort."

"I know," said Laura. "And bottles are hard to get too. We collect old bottles and wash them and scrape off the labels and take them to the hardware store. They give us twenty-five cents for a sackful."

The fruit was chunky and sweet. "Grandpa," said Laura, licking the syrup from her spoon, "tell me about...."

"Aha! I knew it was coming. 'Tell me about the olden days.' Back a hundred years ago, when I was young."

"Yes, but tell me about Mrs. Macdonald—about Lucy Maud."

"Ah, Lucy Maud. She hated the name Lucy, I remember. If you called her *Lucy* Maud, she'd turn her head sharply with her little nose in the air, and her hair would go flying, and she wouldn't speak to you the rest of the day." He sat back, wiped his serviette over his moustache, and chuckled.

"I remember sitting behind her in school. One day I took some strands of her hair and knotted them together. Was she in a state! My chum, Nate Lockhart, was awful sweet on her. He would have done anything to have Maud Montgomery as his sweetheart. But no. No one was going to marry Miss Maud. She was going to be a writer—that's what she always said. She was awfully good at composing, I remember that, even as a young girl. She wrote lovely verses about the sea and adventures of one kind and another, and I remember the excitement the first time she got a poem printed in the Charlottetown paper."

"What did she look like? Was she pretty?"

"Pretty?" Grandpa cocked his head to one side and appeared to be thinking. "I don't know if young Maud was exactly pretty. But she had beautiful long brown hair, I remember, reaching past her waist. She had a small nose and a thin mouth. Her chin came to a tiny peak, and her ears were pointed. She looked a bit like a pixie or a wood elf, especially when her eyes got a dreamy look in them." Grandpa chuckled to himself as he spooned up the last of his fruit.

"Why are you laughing?" asked Laura.

"I'm remembering again how spirited Maud could be when her temper got the better of her."

Laura leaned forward, smiling eagerly. "What did she do?"

"Well, we had the custom of bringing little bottles of milk to school to drink with our lunch. Of course there were no refrigerators in those days to keep the milk cold, so we placed our bottles in the little brook that ran alongside the school. The running stream kept the milk cool. Then at lunchtime we'd all go whooping down to the brook to collect our bottles of milk and go off and enjoy our lunch. But poor Maud wasn't allowed to stay at school for lunch. For some reason she had to go home to eat. And was she angry about that! She so badly wanted to have a milk bottle to put in the brook and share the lunch hour with the rest of us."

As Grandpa spoke, Laura's mind started to wander. She pictured the little milk bottles with their thick bodies, narrow necks and wide openings nestled in the rocks with a fast flowing stream running over them. But in her daydream the milk wasn't white in colour, it was brown. Chocolate milk. She remembered—how long ago was it? Two years ago when they were ten?—a school trip to a milk factory. The class had seen the milk being poured from huge vats into regular-sized bottles, like the ones they drank from at home. Then they watched as the bottles moved like toy soldiers in an assembly line toward the arm of a big machine that clamped lids on them. And then, at the end of the tour the children had been given samples of chocolate milk in the kind of small bottles that she imagined lay in the Cavendish brook.

After they drank the chocolate milk, the boys had held a contest with the empty bottles, lining them up on fence posts and throwing pebbles into them. Peter got the highest number of pebbles in his bottle.

What fun they could have had in Toronto together, going to movies and riding the streetcar! The only problem was, Peter was—. She leaned her head on her elbow and stared at the shiny dark wood of the tabletop.

"Shortly after my time in Cavendish, Maud went out west to

live with her father," Grandpa was saying. "She was sixteen, I remember. But her stay out there was short-lived, only a year. She didn't get along with the father's new wife, so I heard. But look here, what's happening to you, my Laura? Are you falling asleep on me?"

Laura felt her eyes closing in spite of herself.

"That's enough for today," said Grandpa. "The train trip has tired you out. We'll do the dishes and then it's bedtime."

Chapter Three

The next morning, Laura awoke to the sun flooding in her window. She blinked quickly, then closed her eyes again, trying to hold onto her dream.

Grandpa had been in the dream; she was with him on a harvester out west, riding high through the wheat fields. Then, when she turned to look at him, Grandpa had become Peter. She heard him saying in a clear voice, "Long ago, Laura, it was long ago," and as he spoke the two of them jumped down from the tractor into a vast expanse of water. The swirling foam had risen to her neck; everywhere she looked there was nothing but water. Again she heard Grandpa's voice: "The water is fine, but oh, the red soil of the Island is finer. Back home is where my heart is."

Then Grandpa's voice became Peter's again, although she could no longer see him in the waves. He went on and on about the seaweed smell of the sea and the yarns that people told when they gathered in the village store or on front verandahs. He talked about the fun on sleigh rides and the fiddle music that filled farmhouses on Saturday nights and how they would push back the furniture and dance the night away. She was struggling to get out of the water.

One eye opened and then the other. As she lay looking at the gleaming white curtains, she wondered why Peter and Grandpa merged in her dream..

It was no use. Her dream had vanished. She reached for her book on the bedside table, began to leaf through it, and then turned to the last page. Reading the last page was something she often did when she was in the middle of a book. This sometimes spoiled the story, but it felt soothing to read the end of this book, because in the final sentences the author talked about how everyone looked forward to the coming of spring.

She heard voices in the hall downstairs.

"I'm glad she's sleeping late, but I would have liked to at least say good morning to her," she heard her grandfather say. "I can't wait any longer. On my way to the hospital I'll drop by the West Toronto station and send her mother a telegram to let her know Laura arrived safely. Tell Laura I'll see her this afternoon."

Then she heard Bobbie's voice. "Don't worry, Dr. Campbell. You go off before you're late. Laura and I will get on just fine."

Laura stared at the ceiling for a moment. Then, reluctantly, she pushed aside the bedclothes and swung herself out of bed.

Downstairs, Bobbie was dusting the living room furniture with a brown feather duster. A green bandana covered her hair, and she wore a faded apron over her dress. She still wore bright lipstick and her fingernails looked newly polished. She held the duster gingerly. Her diamond ring sparkled. "Well, hello, lazy-bones," she said in a cheery voice when she saw Laura at the door. "Did you have sweet dreams?"

Laura nodded. "I dreamt about Grandpa," she said, hesitating, "when he was young."

"I'll bet your grandpa was a handsome man when he was young, just like my fiancé." She wriggled her diamond ring finger in front of Laura. "He enlisted a few months ago. He's called a private. They'll be sending him any day now to England. Just like your dad, so your grandpa says. It scares me to think of it." She lay down the duster and wiped her hands on her apron. "But I shouldn't worry! I really am proud of him, it's just that...." She put her arm around Laura's shoulders. "But come on into the kitchen now. I'll make you some toast."

"Why did Grandpa leave so early?" asked Laura when she was seated in the kitchen nook.

"Nine o'clock, my dear girl, is not early. "At nine o'clock some people have been up for hours."

Laura said nothing as Bobbie served her toast and peanut butter. She wondered what she would do to pass the day.

"He's usually up and out of here by eight. He stayed later today, but he didn't want to wake you and he couldn't wait any longer." She poured herself a cup of coffee and sat down across from Laura. "I told your grandfather that you'd be welcome to help me clean house...." She smiled broadly. "I hope you know I'm teasing. Anyway, just help me do up these dishes and then you can amuse yourself anyway you like."

After they had finished doing the dishes and Bobbie returned to her dusting, Laura put on a jacket and went outside. She walked around the house, picking her way through a tangle of garden hose, and then sat on the front doorstep. A crisp morning wind cut through the sunshine, and she pulled her jacket tightly around her. She drew her feet up under her so that the skirt of her dress covered most of her legs. Sam bounded over to her and she stroked his ears. His tail wagged as he settled himself beside her.

Across the street, a woman was drawing a rake through the small green shoots of the lawn. Occasionally she bent over a rock garden surrounding an oak tree, and then resumed, moving the rake in short, jerky movements. Laura watched her for a moment, and then slowly got up and walked toward the gate. Sam trotted beside her. She held onto the gate with both hands, continuing to watch as the woman worked.

The woman held herself rather stiffly as she drew the rake toward her, her hands covered with a pair of gardening gloves. A hairnet covered her dark grey hair and she wore small rimless glasses. This old woman couldn't have written *The Story Girl*. She would have no idea what it was like to be young and full of fun. Grandpa must have mistaken her for someone else.

As she watched, the woman seemed to fall forward. She caught herself on the rake, then staggered over to the tree, clutching the trunk. Without thinking, Laura pushed open the gate and ran across the road.

She caught the woman just as she was falling over, and with one arm around her waist and the other holding her arm, Laura guided her to the front steps of her house. Leaning on the iron railing, the woman sat down on the top step. Laura sat beside her. A strand of hair had come loose from under the woman's hairnet and had fallen over her eyes. As she raised her arm to brush it away, she looked at Laura for the first time.

"You're a godsend," she said. Her voice sounded weary. She had a small mouth and her pallor made the blue veins on her forehead stand out. "I don't know what came over me," she continued. "I thought I had plenty of strength to start the spring clean-up, especially with today's lovely sunshine. Haven't felt much like it until now, and perhaps...." Her thin lips stretched into a slight smile. "Perhaps it's too much for me. Especially the raking. I'll leave it for my son and get to the other work." Grabbing the railing, she heaved herself onto her feet and began to walk slowly along the side of the house, inspecting the plants.

Laura stood up and took a deep breath. Should she offer to help, or should she make her way back to Grandpa's house and read her book? Sam had flopped down at the far end of the flagstone path.

"Would you like some help?" Laura's voice sounded like a squeak.

The woman straightened and smiled outright now. "Why yes, that's very kind of you." She gestured toward the bushes beyond the sidewalk. "You can pick up the twigs and rubbish over there." She lumbered toward the steps and from the top landing picked out a paper bag from among a cluster of materials. She handed it to Laura. "It's amazing the dross that collects here over the winter months and is hidden by the snow. Even dead leaves that I thought we'd gathered up last fall."

Laura stood holding the paper bag, suddenly feeling awkward, and then took another deep breath. "Are you Mrs. Macdonald?" She could hear the shyness in her own voice.

"Yes," the woman said. She was bending over the bushes again, snipping here and there with a pruner in her gloved hand. She said nothing else. There was a sharpness in her voice. Then, as if regaining her politeness, she said, "And what is your name?"

Laura half-turned toward her. "Laura."

Mrs. Macdonald dropped her pruner, took off her gloves, and walked toward Laura, extending her right hand. Her face looked surprised and pleased. Her hand was slender, the nails short and well-tended. Laura took it timidly, not used to grown-ups shaking hands with her.

"I didn't think they called young girls 'Laura' nowadays," said Mrs. Macdonald, holding Laura's hand in a firm grasp. "It's a name that belongs to the last century. When was the last time I heard someone called Laura? Several moons ago, let me tell you. I had a dear friend once whose name was Laura. Laura Pritchard. She was a few years older than you when I knew her. Laura was such a sweet girl. Very pretty too. We had such jolly times." Her face was animated now. "She had a brother named Will. Poor, dear Will...." Her voice trailed off. She looked at Laura closely, squinting a bit. "As a matter of fact, you look a bit like my Laura. You don't have a brother Will do you?" She laughed outright now.

Laura shook her head. "I don't have any brothers or sisters."

"Thank heaven for that. Much as I loved her, it would never do for you to be another Laura Pritchard." Her face sobered again and she turned to walk back to where she had been working.

Laura knelt in the soft dirt at the head of a line of bushes. A moment later she heard Mrs. Macdonald's voice again. "I was an only child too. "

There was silence as they continued working, and then Mrs. Macdonald spoke again. "I'm taking advantage of the first days of mild weather this spring. It's almost enough to make you feel alive again. Though goodness knows it will take more than a sunny day...." Her voice faded, and Laura swung around toward her, wondering if she might fall over again. But Mrs.

Macdonald continued to snip the dead flower heads, the pruner working in slow, rhythmic movements. She seemed lost in her own thoughts. "I've always been passionate about my garden. But it's been about four years now—certainly since the beginning of the war—since I've felt much enthusiasm for anything."

Laura continued looking over at Mrs. Macdonald. She seemed to be talking to herself, as if she had forgotten Laura was there.

Laura turned back to the bush again and for a few moments there was silence between them as she struggled to pick up bits of twigs. Her arms brushed against a branch of a rose bush, and she recoiled from the thorns.

"In the book I'm reading, it says spring is infinitely sweeter than you could ever imagine." said Laura.

"What do you mean? Where did you read that? What was the name of the book?" Mrs. Macdonald's sharp tone of voice had returned.

"It's called *The Story Girl*," said Laura. She felt uncertain. She still could hardly believe that Mrs. Macdonald was the author of *The Story Girl* and *Anne of Green Gables* as Grandpa had said. And if she *was* the author, Laura wondered is she had somehow insulted her.

"That's nonsense," said Mrs. Macdonald. "I'm so used to having my own words quoted back to me that I don't know what I've written and what others *think* I've written. Besides, those young girls belong to a past that's over and done. I want nothing to do with them. Sara Stanley, Emily, Anne, Kilmeny—I can't tell you how sick and tired I am." She stood up and arched her back. "Oh, the kinks of old age," she said, wincing. "But you don't want to hear my troubles. Tell me about yourself, Laura.

Are you visiting across the street?"

"Yes," said Laura. "I came here yesterday. I live in Rocky Falls. My school's been closed because of the spring flood."

"And what brings you here, of all places? Why are you visiting Toronto? This city is nothing but cars and noise and too many people."

"It was the only place for me to go," said Laura. "My grand-father...."

"Where are your parents?" Mrs. Macdonald pressed on.

"My mother works in a factory and my dad's gone over to England with the R.C.A.F."

"Oh, yes, the war has split up so many families. It causes nothing but destruction. And now the government is asking us to vote for conscription. They're asking *me*, a mother with two sons, whether I want our Canadian boys rounded up so that they can kill and be killed. What kind of a question is that?" Her gloved hand worked the pruner in quick, spasmodic movements.

"What do you mean?" asked Laura.

"The very thought of it is too upsetting," Mrs. Macdonald replied, her voice shaking. "I can't bear to talk about it."

After several seconds of silence, Laura said, "I'm staying with my grandfather." She waited for a response and then continued, "He knew you." She felt shy and wondered if Mrs. Macdonald was listening.

The snipping sound of Mrs. Macdonald's pruner filled the silence. Finally she spoke. "Where did he know me from?" she asked. Laura looked up to see Mrs. Macdonald squinting at her through her spectacles. "Everyone seems to know me from somewhere," she continued. "I'm weary of people I never heard of coming out of the woodwork as long lost friends."

"He knew you from Prince Edward Island. He went to school with you. He put your hair in a knot once."

Again there was the flash of a smile. "Oh he did, did he?" She looked more closely over at Laura. "And what was his name?"

"His last name is Campbell. His first name is Richard."

"Ah yes, I remember now. I think he was a distant relative of Uncle John Campbell. Well, well, so you're his granddaughter. Well I'll be! And what does Richard Campbell do?"

"He's a doctor too, like my dad," said Laura.

"Yes, now that you mention it, I believe I heard that. He and Nate Lockhart were pals. Goodness me, how long has it been since I've thought about Nate Lockhart? We all did well for ourselves, those of us who came out of that little schoolhouse, each of us in our own way. But tell me, Laura Campbell, do you have any friends here?"

Laura bit her lip. "I have friends," she said, "but not here." She felt her throat tighten.

Mrs. Macdonald stopped working and peered over at her.

"I used to have my friend Peter, but he died last fall," Laura continued. "He was sick for a week, and then he died, just like that." Laura felt the words pouring out of her from a dark place deep inside herself.

Mrs. Macdonald took a half step toward her. "Then you know what it means to lose someone dear to you. You have a sensitive nature. I had a feeling, young as you are, that you would understand something of what I've been through."

"What do you mean?" asked Laura.

"I mean that I think you're—well, to use a phrase you might be familiar with—I think you're a 'kindred spirit'." Mrs. Macdonald leaned on the iron railing and took off her gloves. Laura noticed the thin gold wedding band on her left hand.

"I remember that from *Anne of Green Gables*!" said Laura. "Anne said that she and Diana were 'kindred spirits'."

"And what do you think is meant by 'kindred spirits'"?

"It means that two people are friends, and that they can tell things to each other that maybe they can't tell to other people."

"Yes, that's pretty much what I meant when I first used those words. People who are kindred souls really understand each other."

"I remember that Anne also said that Diana was her 'bosom friend'. Does that mean the same thing?"

"Almost, except that a 'bosom friend' is usually someone you've known a long time. By the way, do you know the name I first gave Anne's best friend, before I decided to name her Diana?"

Laura shook her head.

"I first named her Laura."

Laura gave a start. "You did?"

Mrs. Macdonald smiled and nodded. "After my own friend, Laura Pritchard. In my mind, Diana was kind and sweet-tempered and yet fun-loving, much like dear Laura."

Just then a man's voice sounded through an open window. It began as a low moan and then continued in a strange crescendo.

"I have to go in and see to Mr. Macdonald." With quick movements, as if her own pains had suddenly disappeared, Mrs. Macdonald mounted the steps. "Don't go," she called back just before closing the door. "I won't be a moment. Please stay and keep me company."

Chapter Four

Laura sat on the step and fingered the iron railing. Sam loped up the path and put his head in her lap.

Soon the door opened and Mrs. Macdonald reappeared. She carried a small wooden tray with a glass of milk and a plate of cookies.

"I can't invite you in just now," she said.

Laura sprang up to close the door. As she did so, she got a glimpse of the interior, a half-lit hallway, where a figure, almost a shadow, shuffled about.

Together they sat side by side on the step. Mrs. Macdonald put the tray between them and handed Laura the glass of milk.

"It's good for the bones. You won't tell me, of course, that you don't like milk."

"No, milk is okay," said Laura without enthusiasm. "Thank you," she added, remembering that she was a guest.

"Not as good as lemonade, I'll wager. But better when accompanied by cookies." There was the trace of a smile on her face. "I still make my own. These are ginger cookies. I have a housemaid for the other work. I can barely manage even with that much help, but I do like to bake. Do you like fruitcake? I'll give you a taste of mine one day if you visit me again."

Laura took a bite of her cookie, glad not to have to admit she wasn't a fan of fruitcake. The cookie's sugar coating mingled pleasantly with the sharp taste of ginger and the coolness of the milk. Mrs. Macdonald took a cookie herself and, nibbling absent-mindedly, studied Laura's face. Her eyes were sharp, and Laura felt the woman was sizing her up.

"You seem a sweet girl, my dear and have such lovely thick chestnut hair. How old are you?"

"Twelve. My hair colour is okay but I hate my braids and my bangs. And I hate my freckles and my legs are too long. I'm taller than everyone in my class, even the boys."

For the second time, Mrs. Macdonald laughed outright. The pockets under her eyes disappeared and a slight blush softened the pallor of her skin. For a second, it seemed to Laura that Mrs. Macdonald had become young again, as if she were sitting beside one of her girl friends. "'Ah, vanity, thy name is woman'. It was ever thus," she said, and then leaned forward to study Laura's face again. "Well, you can't change your height or your freckles—which, by the way, are very charming and will disappear eventually. But you *can* change your hairstyle. The braids suit you, but if you don't like them, then change them. Get rid of them."

Laura took a gulp of milk. "I want to do my hair in pincurls, but my mother won't let me."

Again Mrs. Macdonald threw back her head and laughed. "Girls never change," she said, taking another nibble of her cookie. "I dearly wanted bangs when I was your age, but my grandmother was adamantly opposed to new-fangled fashions.

That, of course, was well over fifty years ago."

Laura was intrigued. "You wanted *bangs*?!"

"Well, that was the fashion when I was young. I can still see my grandmother's face when I asked her if I might cut my hair that way. Her face could look very stern sometimes. She drew herself up straight and her mouth became a thin little line, and she looked down at me with her sharp eyes. I knew right away what her answer would be." She shook her head, her smile fading.

"Why did you ask your grandmother?" asked Laura. "Why didn't you ask your mother?"

Mrs. Macdonald swallowed and there was a moment of silence before she answered. "My mother died of tuberculosis when I was very young."

Laura ate her cookie in silence, not knowing what to say.

"My father went out west to Saskatchewan shortly afterwards," Mrs. Macdonald continued, "and my mother's parents, Grandma and Grandpa Macneill, brought me up. They had a farm in Cavendish, and my grandfather ran the post office. Our old house is now long gone. Up until my grandmother's death, it was the only home I ever knew."

"You don't even remember what your mother was like?" asked Laura.

"I remember seeing her in the coffin. Mind you, I was less than two years old at the time, but such a memory stays sharp and clear. My father lifted me up to see her, and I remember her white face and the dark eyelashes that rested on her cheeks. And then I remember a woman's voice in the distance saying, 'Poor little thing.' It was many years before I realized that woman was referring to me."

Mrs. Macdonald had been looking down as though inspecting a sprout of grass among the flagstones, and she now looked up into the distance. "I think one never quite becomes accustomed to losing a parent at a young age. Oh, certainly, one grows up and learns to adjust, but there remains a longing that lasts a lifetime." She picked up the plate to offer Laura another cookie.

"Did you get along with your grandparents?" Laura asked, taking another cookie.

"Oh, they were affectionate in their own way. But they were very strict, as I'm sure I would be if I had a youngster living with me now. They believed in hard work and sober living. I remember having to wear high-buttoned shoes in warm weather when everyone else went barefoot."

"And Grandpa said you had to go home for lunch and couldn't put your milk bottle in the brook to keep it cool like the other kids did...."

Mrs. Macdonald seemed surprised. "He remembered that, did he?" she said, looking up at Laura. "Oh, the humiliations! I remember on Sundays, the dreariest day of the week, we went to church and then we had to sit around in our best clothes reading the Bible. We could read nothing else, and we certainly didn't play outside the whole day."

"I wear my good clothes on Sundays, but I can still ride my bike and I play with my friends when we get home," said Laura.

"Goodness sakes alive! Such activity would have led to damnation in my day! Luckily, on the other six days of the week, I had the most wonderful freedom to explore the seashore and the woods and orchards." Mrs. Macdonald stood up. "Back to work for me. Do you still want to help?"

Laura downed the remainder of her milk and put the glass

back on the tray. Mrs. Macdonald had already pulled her gardening gloves back on. "I'm going to tackle the spirea and the pearl bush," she said. She picked up her pruner and headed for the bushes lining the front of the house. "Do you have a garden at home?"

Laura shook her head. "Not really. My father plants potatoes and turnips and other vegetables. But we don't have a garden like you have."

"I couldn't live without my garden. My perennials and flowering bushes—all my plants, actually—they've always been like dear friends. And look—snowdrops!"

Laura knelt, looking where Mrs. Macdonald was pointing. Small green shoots with the beginnings of white buds nestled in the earth beneath the bushes. The dirt felt rough on her knees.

"What a joy to see a sign of new life. There's so little of it around these days," said Mrs. Macdonald, straightening. She sighed deeply. "Mr. Macdonald isn't well. Some days he's better than others. Today isn't one of his better days."

"Grandpa told me he's sick," said Laura.

"Oh, I'm sure there are all kinds of rumours about my poor husband. He's a minister, you know. He no longer preaches, but his mind still churns dreadfully. He has a mental illness, Laura, and it can't be helped. It's a terrible thing to live with, for him and for me as well. Sometimes I feel that my condition is worse than his."

"Do you have any children?" asked Laura.

"Two sons. Chester and Stuart. Both young men now. And I have two grandchildren. She straightened up, and Laura saw that the hand holding the pruner had begun to shake. "Take this from me, would you?"

Carefully, Laura took hold of the pruner and placed it on the ground. "I think I need to sit down again. Would you mind helping me over to the steps?"

Holding Mrs. Macdonald by the arm, Laura took small paces toward the steps. Beside her, Mrs. Macdonald's body felt heavy and slow. She grabbed the railing and dropped herself onto the step. Laura sat beside her.

"These spells have a way of taking hold of me," said Mrs. Macdonald momentarily. "It's my nerves." The shaking had begun to diminish. "It's good to speak of other things. Tell me about yourself, Laura. Tell me about Peter. He wasn't your boyfriend, was he? I think you're a little young for such things yet."

Laura felt her face flush. "He was just a friend. But he was my best friend. He had red hair and freckles, but they weren't ugly freckles like mine, they were handsome freckles."

"Sounds like Will Pritchard. Red hair. Hazel eyes. Go on. Was he clever in school? Did he tease you? Was he an athlete? What was his family like? What made him such a kindred spirit?"

"Well, he teased me a lot, in a nice way, though. He liked to act—to pretend he was other people. He imitated the mayor of our town, the way he stuck out his stomach and put his hands in his vest pocket, like this." And Laura stood up and strutted down the sidewalk, her back arched, her lip extended. "And he was smart in school. He could add and subtract and multiply in his head, without writing it down. He learned the Morse Code, too. Our school principal said that you might be called to help the war effort if you knew the Morse Code."

"And did you learn the Morse Code as well?"

"No. I wanted to, but only boys were taught. The station

agent taught them. And then Peter started teaching me."

For a moment, Mrs. Macdonald faded from view and Laura remembered the Saturdays afternoons in the back room of the grocery store run by Peter's father. She could still see Peter's freckled hand below a faded shirt cuff tapping out the dots and dashes on an orange crate with the blunt end of a pencil. She could still see the concentrated look on his face, his tongue working at the corner of his mouth. "This says, 'Come back tomorrow'," he said, tapping the staccato of the dots and gentle thuds of the dashes, gradually transforming them into words.

"But I didn't get a chance to learn much..." said Laura. She took a deep breath. "Because he died. Just like that."

"Struck down so young. Poor Will. It happened to him too." Mrs. Macdonald's arm was now still again.

Laura continued, "We used to make snow forts in the winter, and go skating every day after school, and tobogganing on Jackson's hill down by the railroad station. We did that every day when there was snow. And sometimes Jennifer and Wendy came with us, and David and the other boys. But last winter there was just Jennifer and Wendy and me. We used Peter's toboggan. Peter's mother gave it to us." Sam had settled himself at Laura's feet, and she reached down to stroke his head, glad of his comforting presence.

"So then Peter was with you in spirit when you went down that hill on his toboggan. A truly fine way of keeping kindred spirits alive. My cousin Frederica died over twenty years ago. We called her Frede. She was also my best friend. I still feel grief over her death. The same goes for all those other deaths— my father, my dear little son Hugh. He came between Chester and Stuart and was alive for only a few hours. And oh, all those other dear ones—my dear aunts and uncles, especially dear Aunt Annie, and Will, and, yes—and Herman." She smiled again and pulled herself to her feet. "My oh my, dear Laura, you have me thinking about ghosts from my past that I haven't thought of for many a month. To think I should bring up Herman's name, of all people!"

Laura stood up. "Was he your boyfriend?"

Mrs. Macdonald's white hand, the gold wedding band flashing, fluttered up to her face. In delicate motions, her fingertips swept back some strands of hair. "We didn't use the expression 'boyfriend' in those days, but.... Pick up the tray for me, will you please? One of these fine days I'll tell you. Tomorrow, even. Now I must go inside. Mary is fixing our dinner, and I must see how she's getting along."

Laura picked up the tray from the step and handed it to Mrs. Macdonald. She disappeared inside the house, and Laura was once again alone with Sam.

✧

At supper that evening, Laura told her grandfather about her encounter with Mrs. Macdonald.

"I like her, Grandpa. But she seems kind of sad and lonely. And she has shaky hands."

"She may have to take certain medicines to keep her nerves in check. Poor Maud."

"She told me about when she was young, and she even laughed a few times!"

"What did she tell you?"

"She said she wanted to wear bangs, and her grandmother wouldn't let her."

Grandpa chuckled. "Well now, that's the way with youngsters. Always wanting things different from what they are. Her grandmother was quite protective, as I recall. She treated her like a child. She had to wear those pinafore aprons, long after the other young girls were wearing more grown-up clothes. But none of that prevented Maud from making her mark."

They were sitting in the kitchen nook, surrounded on three sides by windows. On the windowsills, African violets were in flower. A poinsettia, still in bloom, sat in one corner.

"It may have been a bit lonely for the poor girl living with her two grandparents, but she wasn't lacking companionship. She had cousins in Park Corner, where she used to visit, I remember that. That was at the house of her Uncle John Campbell, who was a distant relative of mine, and her Aunt Annie, her mother's sister." Grandpa wiped his mouth with his napkin. "And of course she had many friends in Cavendish. She was a good storyteller; she could keep people spellbound for ages. And I think I mentioned to you, Nate Lockhart liked her a lot that year."

"She invited me back to help her with her garden," said Laura.

Her grandfather looked at his watch. "Now you and I will do up these dishes. After that, it's the eight o'clock news. Can't miss that. There's been talk that the Allies are looking for ways to get over to France. A western front. It has to happen sooner or later if we're going to win this war." He pushed away from the table, tight-lipped. "Our Canadian boys will be seeing real action soon."

"Oh, Grandpa," asked Laura, suddenly remembering a question she wanted to ask. What's...." She struggled to get the word right. "What's conscrip....? It has something to do with the war. Mrs. Macdonald is worried about it."

"Conscription." Grandpa ran the water in the sink as Laura gathered the dishes together. "Conscription means that the government has the right to demand all able-bodied men join the armed forces whether they want to or not. To settle the question, our Prime Minister, Mackenzie King, has called a plebiscite. That's a vote. Next week everyone in Canada will be able to say yes or no, depending on whether they think conscription is a good idea or not."

"I guess Mrs. Macdonald is worried that her sons will be made to go and fight."

Grandpa nodded. "I can see why. Her younger son is a doctor. I see him from time to time. He'd be put to good use in the medical corps." He smiled at Laura as he watched her drying a plate. "As for you, young lady," he said, "just be thankful that the only thing you're being called up to do is to help prepare a garden for spring planting."

Chapter Five

The next morning Laura was up before her grandfather left the house.

"Come and walk me to the streetcar, Laura," her grandfather said as he fastened his tie and opened the hall closet. Laura jumped up from the breakfast nook.

"Another beautiful day," he said as they headed down the street with Sam padding along ahead. The street felt like a country road, narrow and winding, and without sidewalks. On both sides, lawns stretched back into groupings of pines and oaks, behind which stood the houses. Some of them seemed as big as mansions. The windows glinted with the reflection of the early morning sun. The mild spring wind brushed Laura's bare legs.

"Unseasonably warm, the forecast says," Grandpa continued. "A perfect day for Niagara Falls. Today's Saturday, so I have early hospital rounds, and then we can spend the rest of the day together. What do you say to that?"

Laura turned to her grandfather. "Niagara Falls! Can we really go?"

"Of course. We'll take the boat to Port Dalhousie, on the

other side of the lake, then a rail car will take us along the gorge to the Falls. Of course, if we were to drive, it would take longer, because we'd have to go all around Lake Ontario to get there."

"But...."

"What is it?"

"Well, I sort of promised—I think Mrs. Macdonald could use some help in her garden."

"You can help Maud until I get back." He looked down at her. "What's so fascinating about Maud and her garden?"

"I don't know. I guess she's just a kindred spirit. Do you know about...."

"Yes, I know all about kindred spirits," Grandpa laughed.

"She started telling me about how it was when she was a girl. She's going to tell me more today."

"You might learn something about gardening from her too," said Grandpa. "Besides being a writer, she has a reputation for being a fine gardener as well. If you'd be relying on me, you wouldn't learn much about gardening. Never did get the hang of it."

At Bloor Street, Grandpa boarded the streetcar and waved Laura good-bye from the window. Laura turned back, with Sam at her heels, to climb the hill leading to the winding street. A horse-drawn Canada Bread wagon passed her, the horse bobbing its head. Sam bounded ahead to keep pace with the horse. The wagon stopped just ahead of her, and the driver jumped out, a wicker basket full of bread over his arm. He waved at Laura as he walked toward one of the houses.

She was reminded of the times she helped Peter with his paper route, cycling from house to house. Their bike carriers would be laden with the folded newspapers. Rather than getting off his bike to take a paper to each house, Peter would pick one up from the carrier while balancing himself on the seat, make an arc with his arm and aim the paper at the mat on the front verandah. The papers nearly always hit their mark.

When the Macdonalds' house came into view, she realized that somehow it didn't look as forbidding as it did yesterday. She remembered the light in Mrs. Macdonald's eyes when she laughed. She wondered if she should she knock on the door. Maybe Mrs. Macdonald did not really *want* her company. Perhaps she or her husband were sick.

Just then, Mrs. Macdonald appeared at the side of the house. She carried a small spade and a paper bag.

Laura crossed the street with Sam trotting behind her, and as she did, Mrs. Macdonald looked up.

"There's the culprit," she said, waving the spade toward Sam. "This always happens in the spring. The snow disappears, the bulbs start to come up, and who chews them?!" She pointed to Sam.

"Oh, I don't think it was Sam," said Laura, and then realized the foolishness of her response.

"I suppose it could have been any dog on the street. Goodness knows, it's little enough to pay for the company of the dear creatures." She stooped down. "Cats are my favourite, though."

"Would you like me to do that?" Laura asked.

"Thank you, that will save my poor old joints." She handed the spade and bag to Laura. "I must speak to my son about my rheumatism. My younger son is a doctor, you know."

"Yes, Grandpa told me. My dad's a doctor too."

"I'm terrified that they'll call up my Stuart. But we mustn't talk about that now. Otherwise I'll get one of my spells and I won't be able to take advantage of the lovely sunshine to work in my garden."

They began walking toward the back of the house. "Do you think you might follow in your father's footsteps and become a doctor too?" Mrs. Macdonald asked. "Some girls are going in to be doctors these days, and I say good for them."

"Maybe," said Laura, "or maybe a nurse." She handed the spade and bag back to Mrs. Macdonald. "Did you know what you wanted to be when you were my age?"

"I always knew, for as long as I can remember, that I wanted to be a writer. I knew that I wanted it more than anything, more than romance, more than wealth. I knew I could never be happy unless I was writing."

"Is that why you didn't want Nate Lockhart as your boyfriend?"

Mrs. Macdonald stopped still, holding the spade in one hand and the paper bag in the other. "My, my girl, you know too much about me. How did you know about Nate?"

"My grandfather told me."

"Poor Nate, he wanted to marry me! And I was all of fifteen! Nate and I both liked reading, and we exchanged books all the time, and wrote notes to each other when we should have been paying attention to our studies. He was great fun to be with. But then he got too serious." She started walking again, moving onto the graveled driveway that ran along the side of the house. "It began with a foolish superstition we had in Cavendish. If you count the first nine stars for nine continuous nights, the first person of the opposite sex you shake hands with afterwards will be your future husband or wife. Well, didn't Nate announce one day that he'd managed the whole nine nights. But since hand-shaking was very common among young people in those days, it was difficult to know exactly which girl he had shaken hands with first, and I simply could not pry the name out of him."

They had reached the gate leading to the back yard, and Mrs. Macdonald turned aside to let Laura open the gate for her. Again, Laura was surprised by the youthful expression on her smooth face. "Well anyway, he finally told me that I was the girl he shook hands with, and not long afterward he passed me a note in school. I'll never forget asking to leave the room and rushing out under a maple tree to read Nate's note. It turned out to be—my first love letter!" She chuckled as she led the way into the back yard. "But I had no interest in Nate that way, and our friendship was never quite the same afterwards."

Laura followed her, with Sam loping behind. The back yard seemed like a miniature park. There were pine trees and a rock garden and a sweep of lawn sloping into a ravine that was thick with bushes. At the far end of the lawn stood red cedar lawn chairs.

"There," Mrs. Macdonald said, pointing to the chairs. "That's one of the signs of summer coming, when we get the lawn furniture out of storage. Normally it does the heart good to see it coming. But this year—I don't know."

She headed for a garbage can near the furniture, where she deposited the bag, and then continued walking toward the ravine. "Come along, my dear. This, when I'm feeling well, is my bit of heaven. See, through here, you can see the Humber River, and on a very still day, you can hear the faint sound of the water flowing. And through these trees you can get a glimpse of Lake Ontario. There are moments, when I see the expanse of water, I feel I'm back in Cavendish."

Laura craned her neck this way and that, and caught a bit of sun dancing on the distant waters of the lake.

"It's strange," Mrs. Macdonald continued, "as much as I have come to love Ontario—and indeed I do, the pine trees especially—my heart still remains in Cavendish. The Cavendish of the old days, of course. Those days are gone, and each time I go back, there is less and less familiar to me. The generation growing up there now—your generation—doesn't know me. I'm just a lady who lives in Toronto and writes books. But enough of this moaning. Let's get to work." She started toward some garden tools by the house, and then stopped. "I almost forgot. How could I forget to show a kindred spirit my hallowed spot?" She pointed to a round granite rock underneath one of the pine trees. "My cat Lucky is buried under that rock. I had the rock shipped up from my old home place back on the Island. Everyone thought I was crazy to do it, and I'm sure the men on the train who had to lift it didn't thank me. But it's a piece of my childhood home, that old rock, and it gives me great comfort."

She headed across the lawn, pulled on a pair of gardening gloves, and brought out a pruner and a rake. "Now, please, my girl. Let's get to work topping off the dead foliage from the perennials." She handed Laura the pruner. "I'm going to make another try at loosening some of the winter bits from the lawn. We'll soon be seeing violets popping up here and there."

Laura headed for the far end, by the gate, and pulling her dress to one side, knelt with her bare knees in the earth. "Mrs. Macdonald, you didn't always live in Prince Edward Island, did you?" she asked. "I mean as a girl? My grandfather said that you went out west."

"My, he does know a lot about me." She began to drag the

rake through the grass. "Yes, that is true. When I was sixteen I went to live with my father in Prince Albert, Saskatchewan. He was remarried by that time, and he and his wife had a baby boy. They were expecting another baby when I arrived—although I didn't know it at the time. They didn't tell young girls about such things in those days. I suppose they thought that I could help my stepmother with the housework and do some babysitting. I also suppose that my father missed me and wanted to have me with him, but it was a very unhappy year for me." She stopped and leaned on the rake. Laura noticed that her arms began to shake as they had the day before.

"My stepmother and I got along like oil and water. It was dreadful. She expected me to do far more work than I felt was fair. I was taken out of school after the baby was born, to work full time for her." She shook her head.

"Did you make any friends out there?" asked Laura.

She smiled and looked up, gazing beyond the treetops that sloped down to the river. "Indeed I did. My friends were what made my year in Prince Albert worthwhile. The Pritchards, Laura and Will, were two of my best friends. I've told you about them, haven't I? They lived on a farm." Laura looked up to see her smiling. "Will was a terrible tease. We used to exchange notes at school, much as Nate and I had done. And then he took to coming around on spring evenings. I have never seen such long, splendid evenings as we had in Prince Albert that spring. Anyway, I remember one particular Sunday evening. You might laugh at this, but it was our custom to spend Sunday evenings in the parlour, singing hymns. On the Sunday evening I'm speaking of, there were four of us in the parlour—Laura and her beau Andrew, whom she later married, and Will and me. Well,

Laura sat at the little organ, her feet in their black lace-up shoes pumping away on the the pedals—I can see her yet in her lovely blue dress—and Andrew stood just behind, turning the pages for her. His head seemed to get closer and closer to hers with every page. And Will and I sat on the sofa together. Sofas in those days were stiff-backed affairs, and we sat very properly, I in my best Sunday brown dress and Will in his starched collar. There was a space between us for another person to sit down, but not for long!" There was a twinkle in her eye and her face seemed at peace. Her arms were once again still on the handle of the rake.

"Some weeks before, he had taken a gold ring from my middle finger and put it on the little finger of his left hand. So on this particular evening, sitting close to him, I tried getting it back. We got into an arm tussle. 'Give me my ring back!' I kept saying." She made flailing motions with her hands, the rake now resting against her shoulder. "But to tell you the truth I didn't try very hard. I got a secret thrill out of seeing that little ring on Will's finger."

"Did you let him keep it?" asked Laura.

"Well, yes, actually, I did in the end. I also gave him a lock of my hair, and he carved our initials on a tree. Then he suggested that we write each other a ten-year letter. This was one of those sentimental things that young people did in those days. We each wrote a letter to the other and agreed that we wouldn't read the letter until ten years were up. I can still hear him saying, 'Perhaps in ten years we'll read them together.' At any rate, I returned to the Island soon afterwards, but it was surely sad to leave Will and Laura."

"What happened to your ten-year letters?"

Mrs. Macdonald began drawing the rake along the sandy-green lawn in quick motions. "I'll never forget the day a few years later. I received a letter from Laura Pritchard that said Will had caught a bad case of influenza and had died within 48 hours. And then a few days later I received a small package in the mail. In it was my little ring. I sobbed and sobbed when it fell into my hands."

She pawed at the ground with the rake, no longer gathering up debris. Her hands had begun to shake again. "Nowadays, they would be able to treat such diseases." Her voice was low now, and Laura had to strain to hear her. There was a bitter edge to it. "What kills the young men nowadays is not so much disease as the war in Europe. And once the Allies land in France, there will be a terrible slaughter."

Laura sat back on her heels, not sure what to say. She looked up to see Mrs. Macdonald looking closely at her.

"My dear, you're very pale," said Mrs. Macdonald. For a moment there was silence between them. "Your friend Peter," she began, "he died very quickly too. What did he die of?"

"Infantile paralysis," said Laura. She began making circles with the pruner in the hard dirt.

"Oh, my. I've heard that it's also called polio and that it's a disease that strikes the young very quickly." Mrs. Macdonald fell silent again.

The ground felt chilly beneath Laura's hands. She pictured Peter's empty desk the day after he was taken to the hospital. Blue ink that was barely dry dribbled down the sides of his inkwell. A brown ruler and an untidy assortment of looseleaf papers stuck out from under the lid, and at the back of the classroom, the coat hook with his name over it hung bare among the array of jackets and hats along the wall. She remembered seeing his mother leaving the school a few days after the teacher had announced his death, her arms filled with Peter's school things. One of her hands clutched the ruler, an ink eraser, and his pen.

"How are you doing with the perennials?" Mrs. Macdonald's voice brought her back to the present. Laura began snipping again.

After a moment she said, "You had two boyfriends, Nate and Will, when you were still in high school. I hope *I'll* be that popular."

"Don't think that's the best thing that can happen to a girl, not by a long shot. The best thing is for a girl to be able to stand on her own two feet, to be her own person. And by the way, there weren't just two. There was a third." She laughed as she returned the rake to the pile of tools and took up a pruner. "You are a naughty girl for getting me to tell you all these stories. I'm not getting my work done." She plopped down onto her knees beside the back step.

"There was also our teacher. His name was Mr. Mustard. John Mustard. He was in his early twenties, close enough in age to me. Well, he had his eye on me, and my goodness didn't he lead me a merry dance. He was fair-haired, with a wispy blonde moustache, and was terribly awkward. And boring! He knew that Will liked me and I think he got a little jealous. And I did things I'm ashamed of now. I got on my high horse and talked back to him in school, things like that. And to my horror, he began to come over to the house to visit. This is what young men did in those days. I think he wanted to court me."

"Court you?"

"Yes—you know, take me out for walks, to dances, to parties.

He used to come by on Monday evenings when Father was at the town council meeting, and he seemed to stay forever. My stepmother would go to bed and leave me with him, and he would go on and on for the rest of the evening. Once I put the clock ahead so that he thought it was later than it actually was. Conversation with him was a torture. And everyone teased me. Even my father would say at the table, 'Pass the *mustard*, please.' Anyway, Mr. Mustard left at the end of that year to become a minister. Before he left, he asked me if I thought something might develop between us, and I got very haughty and said I didn't think so."

"So that was the end of *that* romance!" said Laura. She was now sitting on the lawn facing Mrs. Macdonald, engrossed in her tale. The grass felt cool and damp beneath her. "Did you have any other boyfriends after that?"

"It was definitely *not* a romance, my dear girl," said Mrs. Macdonald. "I never gave John Mustard a chance. We did renew our acquaintance, though, after I was married and my husband and I moved to Leaskdale, just north of here. He turned out to be quite a distinguished minister. He has never referred to all that nonsense long ago, nor have I."

Mrs. Macdonald got slowly to her feet. "That reminds me," she said. "Time for me to check on things inside. And for you my dear...." She looked up. The sun beat down from a deep blue sky. "Today, let's pretend the garden is in full bloom. It's almost warm enough. How about some lemonade?"

Laura shook her head reluctantly. "No, thank you, I have to go now. Grandpa and I are going to Niagara Falls."

Laura walked toward the gate. As she turned to close the latch, she saw that Mrs. Macdonald was waving her pruner at her.

"Well, another day, then." Her face was set in a look of mock sternness. "You're a wicked girl for making me tell you all these things!" she called.

Laura laughed and waved back at her.

Chapter Six

Laura put down her pen and picked up the letter she had just written to her mother.

Dear Mom,

Guess what? I love being in Toronto!!!

Do you remember how I was afraid I wouldn't make any friends? Well, I've made a friend, and you'll never guess who she is! Her name is Mrs. Macdonald, and she lives across the street from Grandpa, and she's pretty old. BUT, Mom, she's L.M. Montgomery. She's the one who wrote Anne of Green Gables *and* The Story Girl *and a lot of other books. I've been helping her get her garden ready for planting, and she's been telling me about when she was a girl. She was a little bit grumpy at first, but now she's nice.*

And guess what else? Yesterday, Grandpa took me to Niagara Falls!! We took a boat right across Lake Ontario, and then we took a train. The falls made so much noise we heard them before we even saw them. You wouldn't believe how fast the water moves, and there's all kinds of mist. We went on a boat that took us almost right under the falls. It was so exciting! We had to wear big, yellow rain coats with hoods and we got soaked! Grandpa couldn't see because his glasses were all wet. Afterwards, Grandpa bought me a chocolate bar—he said I was on holiday, so it was OK.

Love, Laura

"There's not much to do here on a Sunday afternoon," Grandpa said as Laura folded the letter. "People often go for a walk along the boardwalk if the weather is fine. Would you like to join me? This may be the last day before April showers set in."

Laura looked up and nodded with enthusiasm as she licked the envelope. On the dining room table lay a blue square of air-mail paper. She would write to her father later.

✧

"That's the Palace Pier," Grandpa said as they approached the lakeshore. He pointed to a long building just ahead that seemed to jut into the lake. "The boardwalk extends all the way over to the Palais Royale. They're both dance halls. When you're older, you'll be able to come and dance the night away in one or the other of them."

People of all ages were strolling past them, all dressed in their best clothes. "You should have been here for the Easter parade a couple of weeks ago," said Grandpa. "People came by the thousands, showing off their new spring outfits."

Laura felt proud to be walking beside her grandfather, who looked especially distinguished today in his best dark grey suit and starched white collar. But she was not happy with her own outfit. She felt like a little girl in her pink and grey coat with its sailor-style collar. Her oxfords and short socks seemed old-fashioned. Other girls were dressed in houndstooth coats and penny loafers, and some had even drawn a seam up their legs with a crayon so that it appeared they were wearing nylon stockings. Their hats had feathers and veils, like women's hats, while hers was squat, with a silly little brim.

"That looks like their car," said Grandpa, pointing at a black Ford that was crawling along Lakeshore Boulevard.

"Who is it, Grandpa?" Laura had caught a glimpse of a man and woman. The man was driving.

"I think it's Maud and her husband Ewan. Why they're driving, I don't know. Because of the gas rationing these days, most people are trying not to use their cars. But they probably need a change from that dreary house, and I suppose the only way they can get out is to go for a drive."

"I haven't seen her husband yet," said Laura.

"And you probably won't. Maud's quite protective. She's very devoted to him too, considering...."

"What do you mean?"

"Well now, they're a strange couple. Things haven't worked out well for them."

"I wonder why she married him. You told me she didn't want to get married because she just wanted to be a writer."

"That's right—I suppose she'll have to clear up that mystery for you herself. As it was, Ewan waited five years for Maud to marry him. With her talent for story-telling and her high-spirited personality, Maud could have had almost any fellow she wanted at one time, I'd say. It's odd that she settled on the Reverend Ewan."

"Why did he have to wait so long for her to marry him?"

"Because Maud had to look after her grandmother. After her grandfather died, Maud left her teaching job and went back home. Her grandfather, as I understand it, left the farm to one of his sons, but while the grandmother was alive it was hers to live in. She needed someone with her because she was an old woman by this time. So Maud helped her run the farm, but kept on writing whenever she got the chance. It was during that time that she wrote *Anne of Green Gables*."

They passed a huge structure with archways and pillars. It looked like palaces Laura had seen in movies. "This is the Sunnyside bathing pavilion," said Grandpa. "And just ahead is the swimming tank. On a hot summer day, it's the most popular spot in Toronto."

Along the boardwalk were the empty stalls and deserted amusement rides that Laura had seen from the taxi window. A lone vendor was selling popcorn in red and yellow boxes. Grandpa bought two boxes, handed one to Laura, and they continued strolling as they munched their popcorn.

"Then the Reverend Ewan came along as the Presbyterian minister in Cavendish," he continued, "and one thing and another happened—of course, most of the young people who had grown up with Maud were married by then. I myself had left the Island long before. So there weren't a whole lot of suitors left. And Ewan was a fine young man, so they say. He was well educated, likable, a good conversationalist. They seemed well matched in many ways."

He put some popcorn in his mouth and chewed for a moment. "Very sad that it's turned out this way, with his mental illness," he went on. "You have to hand it to Maud, though, for standing by him. A lot of other women would have had him sent to a mental hospital. She continued writing books, year in and year out, all the while doing the things around the church that were expected of a minister's wife."

Just ahead, the black Ford had stopped beside a building with a sign that read, "Palais Royale". Mrs. Macdonald was leaning against the car, surrounded by a group of women. She was dressed in a fashionable black suit and pale pink blouse. On her hat was attached a black net which fell halfway down her face. As Laura and her grandfather approached, Laura could see that her face was pinched, her mouth twisted. Her arms were shaking and one hand grasped the door handle.

As Laura and Grandpa approached, she seemed to be falling over to one side, and Grandpa sprinted ahead to catch her. The women drew back. Her face was pale behind the black netting, and there were deep circles under her eyes.

She gave a start of recognition when she spotted Laura, and her face relaxed somewhat. "You have no idea how I appreciate the face of a kindred spirit," she said. She tried to straighten her hat, but her hand shook so violently that she brought it down again to her side. "See, this is what fame does to me now. Years ago, I was thrilled to have 'fans'. The more the merrier. Nowadays whenever they approach me I feel the need of a remedy to settle my nerves."

Then she looked at Grandpa, who still held her by the shoulders. "Richard Campbell," she said in a faraway voice. "Laura's grandfather. You've been feeding her all those stories about me." She stood straight and seemed calmer now.

Grandpa let go of her. "There are a lot more stories, Maud," he said, smiling. "I remember many things from my brief stay in Cavendish those many years ago. And I've followed the progress of your career through the years."

"My career!" The words burst out in a bitter explosion. She turned her head to the car window and called, "Ewan!" Her voice sounded like the bleating of a lamb.

Grandpa leaned over to open the car door for her. "Those were the days, Richard," she said as she got in. "They seem nothing but an empty shell now. Shall I see you again soon, Laura?"

Laura nodded and blinked away tears. "Tomorrow. In your backyard."

Mrs. Macdonald looked straight ahead, as if she hadn't heard, and the car pulled slowly away.

Laura and Grandpa turned and began to walk back along the boardwalk. They remained silent, watching the gulls swoop down to the lake.

"I remember when *Anne of Green Gables* was first published," said Grandpa finally. "I was a young doctor at the time, and I was never so proud of Prince Edward Island in my life. I wrote Maud a letter of congratulations." He continued. "In my letter I told her how I remembered the verses she wrote as a girl, and the recitations she made at the school concerts. She was always the star of the show. She wrote me back saying how she was always pleased to hear from an old friend. I still treasure that letter. Maud's fame and success doesn't seem to have gone to her head. She has always remained a simple lass from down home."

"Why is she so sad now, Grandpa?" asked Laura.

"Well, when you begin to grow old, you sometimes wish things could have been different."

"But why?"

"That's life, my dear Laura. Sometimes I wish I could have been a better doctor—I wish I could have helped more people back to health. Perhaps Maud wishes she could have written better books. But, you know, Maud's books have given many people a lot of pleasure. That's something she can be proud of."

For the rest of the day Laura was haunted by Mrs. Macdonald's look of sadness. That night she lay in bed, staring out the window at the glow cast by the street lamp.

Then, propping up her pillow, she turned on the bedside lamp and picked up *The Story Girl*. Laura loved to escape into the world of a book, becoming one of the characters. That was why she loved L.M. Montgomery's books—they each had a girl at the centre of the action, and Laura nearly always felt she *was* that girl. But with *The Story Girl*, she didn't feel she was Sara; she wanted to be more like Sara's cousin, Cecily. Cecily was kind and gentle. She collected eggs from the hens and gave some of her egg money to a poor neighbour. She had the natural ability and compassion of a nurse, taking quiet charge when her brother Dan became deathly ill from eating poisonous berries.

Cecily's sister Felicity, on the other hand, who was beautiful and popular with the boys, gave a toss of her lovely head and snorted that it was Dan's own fault for being sick. Felicity was a snob as well, having slapped the ears of the hired farm boy who tried to kiss her—not because he tried to kiss her, but because he was 'beneath her'. Laura closed the book and soon drifted off, imagining herself dressed in a nurse's uniform moving down the long line of beds in her father's hospital in England, soothing the wounded soldiers and airmen and relieving their pain with gentle hands.

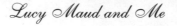

❖

The next morning she was awakened by the aroma of pancakes frying. Downstairs, Bobbie was pouring batter into the frying pan while Grandpa read the paper. Laura watched the pancakes sizzle as she stood by the stove.

"Things are heating up in the east," her grandfather said, turning the page and folding it over. "Heavy bombing in Burma. Mountbatten is—"

"Oh, why don't they all just stop fighting," said Bobbie, the sharpness in her voice contrasting with the prettiness of her appearance. She flipped a pancake onto a plate and handed it to Laura. "Eat up now, so we can get the dishes done and do the laundry."

Grandpa put his paper down. "I told Bobbie that you might help her with the washing this morning, Laura. Do you think you could manage it?"

Laura poured maple syrup onto her pancakes and took a bite. "Well—I thought Mrs. Macdonald could use some help in the garden again."

Her grandfather shook his head, a look of concern on his face. "Poor Maud. I wonder if she's over that attack she had yesterday."

"Can we go to the library too, Grandpa?" asked Laura. "I'm nearly finished my book."

Grandpa looked at her over the top of his glasses. There was a twinkle in his eye. "Is this bribery? 'I'll do the laundry if you'll take me to the library'?"

Laura's face burned. "No, I didn't mean...."

Grandpa laughed as he folded the paper and stood up to

leave. "Of course. We'll go to the library on Saturday."

"I'd help with the laundry anyway, even if we didn't go to the library," she called after him, trying to redeem herself.

After he had left, Laura helped Bobbie with the dishes and then followed her to the basement, each with an armful of sheets and towels. Bobbie set up the washing machine, measured the soap flakes, and began to fill it with water from a hose connected to a tap on the wall.

"Damn war," she said suddenly. "Andy got his papers. He's going to Halifax, then overseas. We were supposed to be getting married before he goes, but now he says he wants to wait." She piled the sheets and towels into the machine. The throttle churned the water. The laundry swished back and forth. "Here, poke it down." She handed Laura a wooden stick.

Laura poked the laundry, her eyes on the swirl of suds. "When is he going?" she asked.

"This week. Just got a letter this morning before I left home. I read it on the streetcar. He didn't even sign it 'love' this time." She banged the rinsing tub in place beside the washer. "I wouldn't be surprised if—well, I shouldn't say it, but I wouldn't be surprised if he asked for his ring back. I'm not sure he wants to marry me any more."

Laura felt awkward.

"I'll show him," said Bobbie to herself, as if Laura wasn't there. She squared her shoulders and turned the tap to fill the rinse tub. "If he wants to leave me high and dry, let him. I'll get along just fine."

"Sure you will," said Laura. She tried to sound encouraging, but it was all so grown up and suddenly she felt like a child.

Bobbie smiled at Laura and reached over to take the stick

from her. "You're so sweet. It's been good to talk to you. I can manage with the rest if you want to go across the street."

Laura made a move for the stairs. "Well, I *did* promise Mrs. Macdonald."

She left Bobbie holding the wooden stick and gazing into the washing machine.

Chapter Seven

Outside, Laura pulled her jacket tight and did up the buttons, then walked across the street and down the gravelled driveway. She peered through the Macdonalds' back gate.

Mrs. Macdonald was on her knees, bent toward the ground, her back to Laura, wearing a spring coat against the sharp wind. Laura came through the gate and walked a wide circle around her so as to not startle her.

"Well, look who the cat dragged in," Mrs. Macdonald said, looking up. She smiled. Her face seemed composed, her body still, unlike her confused state yesterday. "Isn't that a dreadful expression, 'look who the cat dragged in'? I picked it up from my sons." She shook her head and chuckled, looking down at the clump of earth she held with both hands. Her gloves were black with dirt. "The weather is taking quite a turn. It promises to be rainy and cool for the rest of the week. I want to split some of these perennials and get them replanted today."

"Would you like some help?" asked Laura.

Mrs. Macdonald held the clump toward her. "This is one of the miracles of spring. Phlox. In a few weeks it will be blossoming in all its pale radiance. Its fragrance will be perfuming the air."

Laura took the plant from her. "Pry it apart gently," Mrs. Macdonald continued. "Discard the woody centrepiece, leave the live shoots, and I'll replant it in new ground."

Laura worked at the clump of phlox with her fingers while Mrs. Macdonald turned back to the earth and began to dig with a small trowel. There was a peaceful silence between them.

"I was helping Bobbie do the wash. She's engaged and her boyfriend is going overseas."

Mrs. Macdonald raised one eyebrow. She lifted another clump of earth. A tiny green shoot was visible at the centre. "I was engaged to be married once, long before Mr. Macdonald came along. I ended up breaking the engagement, and I left poor Edwin with very hurt feelings. Still, I simply could not go through with it."

"Weren't you in love with him?" asked Laura.

"No, I was definitely *not* in love. I thought the respect I had for him might deepen into love, but that didn't happen."

"What happened?"

"Well, you see, I had known Edwin for a number of years. After I returned to the Island from Saskatchewan, I went to Prince of Wales College in Charlottetown—came fifth in the entrance exams, by the way, an accomplishment I've always been proud of—and from there went to teach school, in some of the little one-room schoolhouses they had in those days."

"Grandpa has told me about them."

"Yes, it was exhausting work. And I was also trying to write, remember. Writing was my first love. I used to get up at six o'clock in the shivering cold, and I'd wrap a blanket around myself while I scribbled away at my stories for an hour or so before getting ready for school." She picked up the tiny phlox plant that Laura had set down and slid it inside a small hole.

"By this time, of course, I was a young woman, twenty-one years old. I was wearing corsets—those dreadful things that pulled your waist in—and putting my hair up. I was sending away stories and poems to magazines all through Canada and the States. And I'd get many of them back in the mail—rejected, rejected, rejected." She sat back on her heels, looking almost relaxed. "Of course, more and more were getting accepted." She poked her trowel in a dry patch of earth. "On occasional trips to Charlottetown I scanned the magazine racks in bookstores to see if there were any new magazines where I might send my writing."

Laura picked up the pruner from the back steps. "Would you like me to prune the dead stuff from those bushes?" she asked.

When Mrs. Macdonald didn't answer, Laura moved over to the bushes by the rock garden.

"Edwin Simpson and I were second cousins. He was very handsome in his own way, and clever in school. I thought he would become a lawyer or perhaps a college professor. It was a secret engagement, so there was never an engagement ring. The night we were engaged, I remember, I picked a sprig of apple blossoms as a little corsage for myself, and he asked me for it. After we became engaged, I discovered that he was studying to be a Baptist minister. My grandparents would have been horrified had they known, since we were Presbyterians. Also, he had a kind of conceit and arrogance that bothered me. He didn't seem to care for anything I had to say. Well, I became more and more miserable, and I dreaded his letters. Also...."

Her voice trailed off.

Laura looked over at her. She was breathing heavily.

"Are you all right, Mrs. Macdonald?"

She closed her eyes. Her face seemed older than it had a few minutes before. "I was in a dreadful dilemma. You see, I never wanted to marry. All I wanted was to devote my life to my writing. But then, what do you think happened? Around the time Edwin was showing an interest in me, I realized that I wanted to have children.

"In the end, though, I knew I would be miserable if I married Edwin. I wrote him a letter breaking the engagement. He wrote back to me saying he would always love me, and in the letter he enclosed the dried sprig of apple blossoms. And what a state I was in! I thought I would have a nervous breakdown over it— and perhaps indeed I did.

"I must say, though, that part of my reason for breaking my engagement with Edwin was that there was someone else." She was patting down the earth with quick strokes around the delicate shoots.

"Who?" asked Laura, piling some of the garden debris into a potato sack.

Mrs. Macdonald shook her head. "That's tomorrow's story. We've been making a nearly daily occurrence of this business, and we might as well continue. So now, I will take myself inside and then I'll continue out here again till the rain comes. I'll see you tomorrow."

❖

The next morning, Laura woke to the sound of a gentle drizzle outside.

Downstairs, her grandfather was scanning the back page of the newspaper. "That was quite a downpour we had last night," he said. "And more is expected today. Finally. The crops need the rain."

Laura looked at the front page as she ate her breakfast. The only picture was one of Princess Elizabeth. The princess was wearing a suit, the skirt flared and the jacket plain, without shoulder padding. She wore Mary Jane shoes and a hat with a small brim, very much like Laura's. If Princess Elizabeth wore such ordinary clothes, perhaps her own weren't so dowdy after all.

"I think Margaret Rose is going to be the prettier princess," said Bobbie, peering over at the picture while she poured Laura's milk. Laura noticed that Bobbie's eyes looked puffy.

"What are you and Maud planning for the day?" asked Grandpa, folding the newspaper.

"Well, if it's not raining too hard, I'm going to help her replant some of the perennials."

Her grandfather chuckled as he pushed back his chair. "Replant the perennials! You're becoming a real gardener! This is almost as good an education as school. Perhaps that spring flood was just what you needed."

"You might not want to go home," said Bobbie. "Rocky Falls will be pretty dull after Toronto."

"Oh, I don't know. I think Laura misses her mother," said Grandpa.

"I wonder if she got my letter yet," she said.

"She'll get it today for sure. Mail usually takes a day to get to Rocky Falls. So you should get a letter back from her by the end of the week," said Grandpa.

"My friends Jennifer and Wendy said they'd write to me too." She looked out the window for a moment, trying to imagine the things her friends would be doing now that the school was shut down. She could see them in their high rubber boots down by the flooded areas of the town, trying out makeshift rafts with some of the others. She was beginning to feel homesick.

"Have you seen the inside of the house over there?" asked Bobbie.

"Pardon?" asked Laura. Her thoughts were slow in returning to the present.

"The Macdonalds' house."

"Oh—no." Laura had begun to wonder if Mrs. Macdonald would ever invite her inside. The more she talked to her, the more Laura had become curious about the house. She wondered especially where Maud did her writing.

"Well, they're pretty reclusive, the two of them," said Grandpa. "I don't know if you'll get invited in." He looked at his watch. "I wish that I wasn't so busy these days. With more and more of the younger fellows enlisting, it means more patients and more hospital work for us older doctors. Well, it's all part of the cause." He stood up. "Still, I'd like to take you to see a movie one of these days. Saturday perhaps."

The drizzle had stopped by the time Laura got outside, but the sky was still thick with heavy clouds. When she reached the Macdonalds' back gate, she saw that Mrs. Macdonald was already at work at the far end of the yard, near the edge of the ravine, pruning a forsythia bush.

"I'm going to let you clear out some of the mess from the rock garden," she said when she saw Laura. "I'm cutting some forsythia branches to take inside. This is a little trick we call 'forcing the forsythia'. You take the branches inside, put them in a vase and watch them blossom into a lovely bouquet. The blossoms appear more quickly inside than outdoors." She stood straight and looked up at the sky. "It's going to rain again."

Laura knelt in the dirt. The overnight rain had soaked it, making it squishy under her knees. "There are some little green buds down here," she said, bending close to the earth.

"Lily of the valley. It makes wonderful ground cover, and in a month's time, the fragrance will be heavenly."

The two worked together in silence for awhile, their backs to each other. Birds flitted and chirped among the trees. A robin flew down to the lawn near where Laura knelt. The wet thickness of the brush and the trees leading down to the river reminded Laura of a jungle.

"Today is Princess Elizabeth's birthday," Laura said after awhile. "She's sixteen. Her picture's in the paper."

"That girl will be taking on quite a responsibility some day, when she's queen," said Mrs. Macdonald.

"I wish I was sixteen."

"And how old are you?"

"Twelve." Laura pawed the earth beneath her fingers. "I don't like being twelve. I want to be grown up."

"Well, my advice is this: enjoy being twelve years old. You'll be grown up soon enough, and then before you know it you'll be sixty and you'll wonder where your life has gone." She took a heaving breath as she gathered the forsythia branches in her arms.

Laura sat back on her heels and looked over at her. Mrs. Macdonald straightened and turned half-way round. In profile, her features were fine and delicate. She walked over to the back step and set down her armload of branches.

"I'm going to try snipping off all these dead heads before the rain," said Mrs. Macdonald. She pointed to an area beside the back step. "This is my cutting garden. I keep flowers here that I cut to make bouquets for inside the house. White cosmos, I think, is my favourite."

Mrs. Macdonald took up the pruner, and for a few moments Laura heard nothing but the steady sound of snipping.

"While I was still engaged to Edwin, I got a teaching job in a village called Bedeque. I boarded at the Leard farm. Herman was the Leards' son. He was a bit older than I was. He had dark hair with a curl that fell just so over his forehead. One night, coming home with the horse and buggy from a social outing, he put his arm around me. Well, that was it. I fell head over heels for him. There's no other way to describe it. Head over heels. Eventually my head prevailed, thank goodness."

"What happened?" asked Laura. She tried picking at the debris quietly so as not to miss a word.

After a moment, Mrs. Macdonald continued, "He always found ways of being alone with me. One evening, he and I were

alone in the sitting room. He was reading and I was writing a letter. Suddenly he closed his book and said he was tired. I said to him, 'Why don't I read to you?' Silly young woman that I was! So I went over, sat beside him and picked up the book and began to read. Of course, it wasn't long before he took the book from my hands and laid it on the end table...."

Laura looked over at her. Her head was shaking in quick movements and her voice trembled. "I'll never forget...."

Drops of rain began to fall. "Here it comes," said Mrs. Macdonald. She took brisk paces toward the back step, her voice normal again. "Let's get the rubbish into a pile. We're hiring a man to come and do the heavy work."

Together they worked furiously at it as the rain came faster and faster.

Mrs. Macdonald's hair fell in wet strands about her face. "We're getting soaked," she panted.

When they were finished, Laura clutched her jacket tight against herself and sprinted toward the gate. Rain drops were trickling down the back of her neck. "Good-bye, Mrs. Macdonald," she called back.

"Wait, Laura! Where are you going?"

Laura stopped and turned around. Mrs. Macdonald stood bewildered, looking at her through rain-spattered spectacles. "Aren't you coming inside?" Laura blinked the rain away from her eyes and grinned. "Sure!"

Mrs. Macdonald bent down and gathered up the forsythia branches, and together, the two climbed the steps to the back door.

Chapter Eight

Laura followed Mrs. Macdonald through the screen door into the back porch. She kicked off her rubber boots.

"That's the nice thing about big country boots like those," said Mrs. Macdonald, looking down. "No fussing with them."

Inside, the kitchen was spotless and shining. On a corner counter, bread was rising in a big bowl.

"Mary is downstairs doing the ironing," said Mrs. Macdonald, laying down her armful of branches. "I'll get a vase."

She disappeared into the dining room and returned with a large china vase. "Here we are," she said. "These branches with their tiny yellow buds are some of the first signs of spring." She filled the vase with water from the sink and started arranging the forsythia. "I love a large vase of flowers."

Her slender hands worked the branches this way and that, and finally she stood back and looked at the bouquet. "Come," she said, and led the way to the dining room, a panelled room with a heavy dark table and sideboard. "This will give some brightness to the room." She cleared away a bowl from the centre and placed the flowers on the cutwork centrepiece. "Look at this.

The colors match."

The cloth at the centre of the table was embroidered in purple and yellow pansies. The work had been finely done.

"That's pretty needlework," said Laura. "I do the lazy daisy and the stem stitch and that's about all. And cross stitch. The simple stitches. I embroidered a dresser cloth for my mother's birthday."

"I'm glad to hear it. I thought needlework was dying out with my generation. I embroidered this one here," she said, running her hand across the centrepiece, "during one of those difficult years after Grandfather Macneill died. I haven't told you about those years."

Mrs. Macdonald had been looking at Laura over the tops of her wet spectacles. She now took them off and led Laura back into the kitchen. "Take your jacket off and hang it on one of the hooks in the back porch," she said, removing her coat.

"Now, then," she said, her eyes larger and more piercing without her glasses. She stood cleaning them with a hankie. "Now," she repeated. "A glass of milk. And let me see if there are some Boston drop cookies. Sit down here at the table."

Mrs. Macdonald placed the milk and cookies on the table and picked up some knitting from the seat of a chair. Her lips moved as she counted the stitches. The wool was heavy and grey. The work seemed to calm her. She looped the wool over her finger and positioned the needles.

"I haven't finished telling you about Herman," she began. Then her hands began to shake again. She put down her knitting and brought her hands up to her head, trying with agitated fingers to smooth her hair. After a moment her pale face relaxed and once again her hands became quiet. "A telegram came one winter day with the news of my grandfather's death, and my life changed in an instant. I gave up teaching and went home to live with my grandmother. And that was the end of Herman too.

"We weren't a match, anyway. We had very little in common. If I had become further involved with him, it would have been a disaster."

"Did you ever see him again?"

"Only once, the following fall, when I went back to visit. He asked me to go for a walk one evening when he was going to bring in the cows, but I said no. And I never saw him again." She had taken up her knitting again, her fingers moving the wool skillfully.

Laura remained silent. Mrs. Macdonald's eyes were intent on the work in front of her. From another room a clock struck the half-hour, and she could hear from the basement the faint sound of Mary humming a tune.

"I've sometimes had regrets," Mrs. Macdonald said at length. "But not often. I would have made a terrible mess of my life had I married Herman Leard. For one thing, I would have been an early widow."

"What do you mean?"

"One day the following summer, my grandmother said to me, 'Wasn't there a Herman Leard where you boarded over in Bedeque?' 'Yes,' I said. I tried to sound calm, but my heart was racing. Then she told me she'd just read his obituary in the *Pioneer*." She put her knitting down on her lap and held up an imaginary newspaper. "I picked up the paper and there it was. Dead. Influenza. Buried on his twenty-ninth birthday. And do you know what happened to me?"

Laura shook her head.

"All the deaths of my life came rushing up. My father had died a few years before. My grandfathers. Will." Her voice was now barely audible. "And my mother."

Laura's cookie felt like sawdust in her mouth. The rain now pelted against the windows. She was grateful for the sounds of Mary moving around the basement of the silent house. She thought of Peter, and felt a pain in her chest.

"I think I have to go, Mrs. Macdonald," she whispered.

Mrs. Macdonald looked at her with pleading eyes. "How good it is to have you to talk to. You'll come back tomorrow, won't you? Even if it's raining?"

Laura nodded. "Sure I will," she said.

✧

That evening after supper, Laura and Grandpa sat in the living room playing checkers. The checkerboard sat on the coffee table between them.

"My move, I think," said Grandpa, and he raised his hand, made a play, and collected two of Laura's checkers. "You don't seem to be concentrating tonight, Laura," he said. "Usually we're much more of a match than this."

Laura reached out to make a play, then drew her hand back. She sat back in her chair. "Grandpa," she asked, "did you see Mrs. Macdonald again after you left school?"

They began to clear the game away. "I met Maud only twice during those years after I left Cavendish."

"When was that?"

"The first time was after I'd begun studying medicine. I was working in Halifax for the summer and to my surprise I happened to see her on the street one day. She was dressed in a smart grey dress and the kind of big flowered hat that was the fashion for women in those days. Maud always dressed stylishly. Anyway, we stopped and talked for awhile. She told me she was studying at the university there. She also said she was beginning to have some success with her writing. When I asked her about her studies, she replied, 'I've had to fight to get an education, Richard.' I asked her why, but she was in a hurry to get to her classes. So we said good-bye, and I didn't see her after that."

"But you said you saw her twice," said Laura.

"Yes, the other time was many years later when I went back to Cavendish to visit friends. By then I was working as a physician here in Toronto. I'd heard that Maud had returned to Cavendish to care for her grandmother. And of course she had become well known by then as the author of *Anne of Green Gables*. One afternoon I met her walking along a path from the sea. Maud always loved to walk along the seashore. It was a lovely summer's day, I remember. I tipped my hat to her and said, 'Hello, Maud. Do you remember me?' And do you know what she did? She passed me right by! She didn't even look at me. The strange thing was—she was talking to herself, right out loud! It was quite an animated conversation she was having with herself too." He chuckled.

"Didn't she recognize you?" asked Laura.

"She didn't even seem to see me. I was told afterward that when she was out walking she often practised aloud the dialogue between the characters of whatever book she was writing at the time. That's probably what she was doing when I met her. She was completely lost to everything except the conversation she was planning for her book."

"Did people think there was something wrong with her?"

Grandpa shook his head. "Oh, I don't think so. The people of Cavendish knew Maud pretty well. And they were proud of her. I heard too that the publisher never gave her any peace after *Anne of Green Gables* got published. Everyone who read it kept asking, 'What happens to Anne after this?' and so the publisher wanted her to write more and more books about Anne. In fact, she just finished one of the Anne books a few years ago. It's called *Anne of Ingleside*. And of course, as you know, she's written many other books as well." He fumbled with the checkerboard box. "That time I met her on the path in Cavendish—the time she was talking to herself—that was the last I saw of Maud until I discovered we both lived on this street."

✧

The next morning, Grandpa set aside his breakfast plate and morning paper and sat forward, leaning on his elbows. "Laura," he said, "Our conversation about Maud last night made me wonder if she has talked to you about her books."

Laura shook her head. "She got mad when I said something about *The Story Girl* the first day I was over there. She said she was sick and tired of her books and she didn't want to talk about them."

"That surprises me," said her grandfather. "She's received all kinds of honours, you know. She received the Order of the British Empire from the King himself a few years ago."

"She doesn't talk like someone who's famous. She talks just like she's my friend."

"Perhaps it was important for Maud to know that you were

her friend before she talked to you about her books. She knows you now. So why don't you ask her about them?"

"If she doesn't talk about her books, what does she talk about?" asked Bobbie as she came into the kitchen, the grocery list in her hand.

"She talks about the friends she had when she was young," said Laura. "And about her garden. She loves flowers. She loves spring. She said the spring wakes her up. And...."

"Let's see what's on special this week," said Bobbie, picking up the paper from where Grandpa had discarded it. She leaned against the cupboard and began leafing through the pages.

Laura noticed that her left hand was bare. "Bobbie, your ring!" she said, dropping her spoon into her cereal bowl. "Where is it?"

Grandpa put his finger to his mouth to silence her, then shook his head and took a sip of coffee.

Bobbie lowered the paper. "It's on temporary displacement," she said. "It may be permanent. Andy doesn't even want me to come to the station with him. Is that any way to treat your fiancée?" She turned back to the paper. "Maybe he's got another girlfriend. I wouldn't put it past him."

"We're not living in normal times, Bobbie," said Grandpa to the back of the newspaper. He hesitated. "Perhaps you'll feel better if you did your part for the war effort too. Knitting or...."

"Knitting!" The word came out in a muffled explosion.

"Well, even the Queen is knitting socks for the servicemen. She's turned one of the rooms in Buckingham Palace into a work room for women."

"Mrs. Macdonald was knitting something yesterday," said Laura.

They sat in silence for a few moments. The only sounds were Sam's soft snoring as he lay on the mat by the back door and the rustle of the paper as Bobbie turned the pages. Laura had lost her appetite, but tried finishing the last of her cereal looking at the back page of the newspaper in Bobbie's hands. One of the headlines caught her eye: "12 Canadians Missing After Air Operations." Above the headline was a picture of an airman, smiling, looking just as her father had looked when he waved goodbye from the train.

"Grandpa, do you think Dad is all right?" she asked, her voice shaky.

"No reason to think otherwise. You told me the last you heard he was—what are you reading?"

Laura sat halfway out of her chair, peering at the paper's small print. "'The following is a partial list of casualties and next-of-kin....'" she read aloud.

Something inside had turned to lead. What if her father—?

Her grandfather bent over toward where Bobbie stood holding the newspaper in Bobbie's hands. "Laura, no news is always good news," he said quietly. "If this war continues much longer, we'll all have to believe that. We've had no news of your father lately. That means...."

"He's safe?" whispered Laura.

Grandpa nodded. "As far as we know, he's safe. That's all we have to go on, but why imagine the worst?" He looked at his watch and rose from his chair. "Bobbie, get us the best bargains you can with our rationing coupons," he said. His hand rested briefly on Laura's shoulder as he left the kitchen.

Chapter Nine

After Grandpa had gone and Laura had helped Bobbie with the breakfast dishes, she stood at the front door looking out across the street. The morning seemed to have settled into a light misty drizzle. The trees across the street looked bare and dreary.

She opened the door and ambled across the street and up the flagstone path. She stopped when she reached the iron railing that enclosed the front stoop of the Macdonalds' house. A fleeting figure passed in front of one of the upstairs windows. She pulled her jacket tighter around her against the light rain, and just then the door opened a crack and Mary's face appeared.

"She says to come in," the housemaid said in a loud whisper, "only please be quiet because Mr. Macdonald isn't well and mustn't be disturbed."

She looked Laura up and down. "Take your jacket and your boots off and leave them in the vestibule here." She opened the door wider.

Inside, Laura could hear the voices of a man and woman. A man's voice groaned, sounding deep and gruff. Mrs. Macdonald's voice sounded soothing, and then sharp. He responded in a whimper, and then his voice fell quiet.

"She'd like you to help her out in her writing room," said Mary, leading the way toward the stairs. Passing the living room, Laura saw a dark blue sofa and chair, stitched cushions, and a bookcase. On the mantelpiece stood an ornamental jug.

"This way," said Mary when they reached the landing at the top of the stairs. There were several doors, all closed. Mary opened one and led her inside. Facing them, a desk stood against a wall with a large window. Through the window the pine trees of the ravine were visible. The other three walls of the room were lined with books from floor to ceiling. Laura had never seen so many books outside of a library. Even Grandpa, who had more books than anyone she knew, had only two book-cases in his living room.

"The two of them have more books than anyone else in this city," said Mary, echoing Laura's thoughts. Then she disappeared and Laura was alone. She looked around, and immediately her eyes were drawn to the photos on a small table beside the desk. At the centre was a small photo of a young woman. The photo was brown and faded with age, and Laura guessed that it might be Mrs. Macdonald's mother. Beside it was a photo of a distinguished-looking bearded man, perhaps her father. Another one showed a girl about Laura's age with a pixie face and heavy-lidded eyes and hair that was so long it extended down to the girl's waist. The girl looked vaguely like Mrs. Macdonald herself. In a fourth photo, two young women in long black stockings and short shift-type dresses stood smiling. Behind them, ocean waves crashed on rocks. Laura recognized the outfits as old-fashioned bathing suits. She and Jennifer and Wendy had gotten into Wendy's grandmother's trunk one day and had brought out a costume like these. They had taken turns trying it on. She bent to look more closely at the women.

"Admiring my photos, are you?" came a voice from behind.

Laura turned. Mrs. Macdonald stood dressed in a black lace dress, her hair crimped into waves. She looked like she might be going to a tea party. The woman looked down at her skirt, smoothing it in rapid movements. "How do I look?" she asked.

She sat down at her desk, suddenly tired, and indicated to Laura a footstool covered with a needlepoint design. Laura sat down.

"I've been going through my things and trying on my old dresses," Mrs. Macdonald continued. "I haven't worn this dress for years. I'm surprised it still fits. This is the dress I wore to receive the Order of the British Empire. The Order was signed by the old king himself, George V, but of course I received it from the governor-general in Ottawa. I made a pretty curtsy to him." She smiled and raised her hands, which were fluttering about, to her hair.

"Grandpa says you got lots of awards and honours."

"Yes." She looked out the window. "This is by far my favourite spot in the whole house. Look at the view—the pines and flowering bushes, the river and the marvelous green space beyond, and over there, the lake. How fortunate I am!" Laura stood up and bent toward the window to follow her gaze. Outside it still looked dreary.

"Yes," Mrs. Macdonald said again, "I've received several honours through the years. "I don't know what it all means anymore. All I want now is to put my things in order as best I can. I've been sorting through my clothes. I've always liked being well dressed. You should have seen my wedding trousseau! And my wedding gown itself! It's up there, wrapped in tissue paper. It's still a lovely gown, decorated with delicate lace and hand-sewn pearls. Good grief, when I think!" She spread her shaking fingers on either side of her waist. "I had a twenty-two inch waist when I was married. And I wasn't a young woman, either. I was thirty-six years old. Verging on middle age." She patted her stomach, across which stretched the satin and lace of her dress. "All this weight began to appear, oh, I suppose after the birth of my children, but especially so over the past ten or twelve years."

Mrs. Macdonald shook her head slowly back and forth. "It's been thirty years! In some ways it seems like yesterday, the day I walked down those stairs in Uncle John Campbell's house carrying a bouquet of white roses and lily of the valley and saw Ewan waiting for me by the parlour mantelpiece. Sometimes it's–it's like it just happened. "But then other times...." Her mouth became twisted in the way it had on the boardwalk. "Other times...." She turned her head from side to side, her face contorted, her hands clutching the arms of the chair.

To her own surprise, Laura reached out for Mrs. Macdonald's hand. Her gold wedding band felt loose on the thin finger.

"Would you like me to get Mary?" Laura asked.

"No," she whispered. "Just keep on stroking my hand. It brings me peace. It connects me to...." She stopped, and Laura wondered if she might be falling asleep.

After awhile her lips began to move. Her lips were as pale as the rest of her face. "If Ewan hadn't had this strain of mental illness...." She opened her eyes and looked into the distance. "He's been a good man, a decent man."

"Was he a minister in Cavendish? Is that where you met

him?"

"That's exactly what he was." Her voice gained strength as she talked, and her face looked more composed. "He came to Cavendish in 1903 or 1904—a few years after I had come back to live with my grandmother. By that time, of course, I was approaching thirty years of age. All my old chums had either moved away or were married and raising children. I was very happy as a writer, but the fact was that I was alone. And oh my, I dearly wanted children."

"Did he—did he court you?"

She smiled and a hint of pink appeared in her lips. "In a manner of speaking, I suppose he did. It was a rather odd way of courting, however. You see, my grandmother took over the Cavendish post office after my grandfather died, and I was her assistant. Ewan began paying visits to the post office—first of all it was every day, then two and three times a day. People wondered why the minister should have so much business in the post office!"

She smiled at the thought, and then continued. "Well, to be honest, Ewan was a fine man. He was five years older than I was, he was a good conversationalist, he had a pleasant manner and a droll sense of humour. We argued a lot, but it was enjoyable to spend an evening talking with him. I remember thinking to myself one day, 'If he asks me to marry him, I think I'll accept.'"

"And I guess he did!" said Laura.

"Well, I was beginning to wonder. He had announced that he was leaving Cavendish to go on a year's study leave in Scotland. The time was getting closer and closer, and he didn't say anything, and I thought, well, he'll just leave and that will be the end of it. But one evening, when he was driving me home with the horse and buggy after visiting friends, he asked if I would marry him. As I told you, I was prepared for my answer.

"I said, 'I cannot marry you right now because I must stay with my grandmother until she dies. But after that, if you want to marry me, then my answer is yes." I can still hear him—there was a pause, and then he said in a gruff voice, 'I don't want to give you up.' And he waited five long years. After my grandmother died I no longer had a home because my uncle took over the place immediately. There was no reason to wait any longer, and so I married Ewan three months later. We had a long honeymoon in Scotland and England and then came to Ontario."

"Did you ever go back to Prince Edward Island?"

"Only for visits. I never lived there again. But Ontario has been a lovely province to live in. We lived in two pretty little towns before moving to Toronto. We've had splendid holidays up north in the Muskokas. I especially love the pine trees here in Ontario."

"Did your husband keep on working as a minister?"

"Yes, he did. It wasn't an easy life for me. I had to entertain a lot, and I did church work. I organized the young people who put on dramatic productions. I had my two little boys to bring up. And then, of course, I did all the things that housewives had to do in those days—I cooked and baked and cleaned house and made jam and preserves. Of course, we always had a house-maid, but my grandmother had taught me very high standards, and so I insisted on doing a lot of the housework myself. There weren't any modern conveniences like vacuum cleaners and washing machines in those early days, remember, and so it was hard work. And I was also writing books all this time! And then as well...." She paused for breath.

"There was Ewan's condition, his mental illness...." She paused again. "As a minister, of course, Ewan was very prominent in those small towns, and I felt I couldn't let anyone know that he was mentally ill. And so I was forced to keep up a certain front. I succeeded in keeping his condition from the congregation. I don't know how I did it, but it certainly took the stuffing out of me."

"Did you get sick?"

"Well, not exactly sick. My nerves began to bother me. I couldn't sleep. I got upset easily. To tell you the truth, I think I've become worse and worse through the years. I sometimes wonder if *I'm* not the more mentally ill one in the family. And yet I still have to hold everything together, because Ewan can do nothing any more." She stared ahead at the rain-misted window. "And then there are my sons."

"I know one of them's a doctor. You told me that before, and so did Grandpa. Where does he live?"

"Here in Toronto. He's Stuart, my pride and joy. If the majority of Canadians vote in favour of conscription next week, I'm afraid he'll be called up. It worries me terribly."

"Why?" asked Laura.

"'Why?!' Don't you know the dreadful things war does to people?!" Mrs. Macdonald's voice rose and she stared hard at Laura.

"My dad's over there," said Laura quietly.

"So he is," said Mrs. Macdonald, her face softening. "I'd forgotten. I'm sorry, my dear. It's just that when I think of what might happen to Stuart...." She closed her eyes.

"What about your other son?" asked Laura.

"Chester—Chester has brought many disappointments to our lives. And he has ruined his own. He married and had two dear babies, but he and his wife have gone their separate ways. I rarely see the children. I hardly even feel like a grandmother. In the middle of the night, when I hear Ewan groaning and grunting, and my nerves are so frayed I feel I can't hold myself together a moment longer, I think, 'What have I done to my sons? What could I have done differently?'"

She smiled over at Laura. "Looking at you now, I wish I'd had a daughter. But then, if you were my daughter, I'd worry about you too—about your studies and about what kind of friends you have and what kind of world you'll be living in after this war is over."

Laura looked at the photos on the table beside the desk. "Do you have any pictures of your grandchildren?"

"There must be some around somewhere. But I keep these photos here to remind myself of days gone by—old times and old friends. Memories are what keep me going. And, of course, my garden." She smiled again at Laura. "And I mustn't forget new friends who have become kindred spirits."

"Are we going to do any work today?" asked Laura. The room felt cool, and she tucked her legs under her skirt.

After a few moments when Mrs. Macdonald was still silent, Laura asked again, "Do you need any help up here?"

Mrs. Macdonald shook her head. "Not today, my girl. I think I'll stay with my memories—my *good* memories—a bit longer. I'll see you tomorrow."

Chapter Ten

"I'm much better today, my dear," said Mrs. Macdonald over her shoulder as she led Laura up the stairs the next day. "I wouldn't have ever thought it, but I actually got a good night's sleep last night. I was waiting for a ray of sunshine in this unremitting rain, and lo and behold, here you are," she said, opening the door of her writing room. "So I have the best of both worlds. We need the rain for the flowers and the trees and the lawns if the promise of spring is to be fulfilled. It's one of those facts of life." She closed the door behind them .

"I'll tell you what I want you to do today," she continued, sitting down at her desk. "I want you to help me get together my books. I'm sorting what is mine and what is Ewan's. Don't ask me why." She seemed to have regained colour in her face and hands since yesterday.

"I've been collecting stories from my early career," she said, holding up a sheaf of papers. "Stories from, here, there and everywhere. I've been putting them together to get published."

She put them down again and stood surveying her shelves, turning this way and that. "Where do I start?"

"Why not start with your own books?" asked Laura. "The books you've written, I mean."

"Oh, yes," Mrs. Macdonald replied, laughing. "They're down there. On those bottom shelves. All bunched in together. They don't stand on display like trophies."

Laura squatted down to look at the books. There they were on three long shelves, one title after another, written by L.M. Montgomery. Most of the books Laura had never heard of. She twisted her neck to get a better look at the titles. "*Kilmeny of the Orchard, A Tangled Web, Magic for Marigold, Jane of Lantern Hill, Pat of Silver Bush....*" She read them aloud.

"Nearly every title has the name of a girl," said Mrs. Macdonald. "Why did this happen? I'm not sure. Perhaps I wanted to keep on writing about the joys of my own girlhood. After all, there is nothing more lovely than to see oneself at the beginning of life and imagine all the beautiful things that might lie ahead."

"Was it easy for you to write books?" asked Laura. She moved over to sit on the footstool. "I mean, did you just sit down and make up the stories? I can't imagine writing all these books."

"I've always begun by doing what I call 'spade work'. You know how you get a garden ready by pruning the plants and preparing the soil—the kind of thing we did together earlier this week? I've done the same kind of thing before writing a book. I plotted the story line and developed characters. I listened carefully to stories that I heard people tell and I jotted them down in a notebook. I tried to imagine conversations. People have told me that I seem to be talking to myself when I'm working out my characters' dialogue. Sometimes I even catch myself doing that."

Laura opened her mouth to tell her about Grandpa's experience meeting her on the path in Cavendish, then decided against it.

"The writing, once I started, went along smoothly enough. The trouble was finding the time to write. I think I told you that in the days long ago when I was teaching school, I got up early in the morning to write. Then, when I lived with my grandmother during those years, I often wrote in the evenings after the housework and my post office duties were over for the day. I wrote by the light of an oil lamp, of course. We didn't have electricity in those days."

"Where did you get the ideas for so many books?"

"Oh, I was never lacking ideas. Sometimes an item in the newspaper sparked an idea, and I'd jot it down in my notebook. Once my imagination gets going, it knows no limits in thinking up characters and plots."

"My friend Wendy writes poetry and stories. She wrote a Hallowe'en story about a friendly witch last year that won a prize for the whole county. She said the idea just came to her from nowhere. She has a diary too, and she writes in it every day. I don't think I could think of enough things to write about every single day."

"You find that many interesting things happen in the course of a day once you start writing about them. Your friend has the right idea. It's important to observe the details of what goes on every day. I began a journal when I was not much older than you, and I have written in it all these years. It now fills several volumes. I enjoy going back to read what I wrote in those early years, and I laugh a bit over some of the things that I thought were a matter of life-and-death."

"The things you wrote when you were a girl—did you show them to your friends? Wendy never lets me read the poems she writes."

"Well, yes, I can understand why. When you start writing poetry, you're often unsure of yourself and you try out other people's styles. Then you read it over and it seems silly and forced because it's not your own style. I remember, once, writing a poem about peaches and pears, which I hardly ever had the chance to eat. The poem also had a sportsman's horn in it, and I'm not sure I even knew what a sportsman's horn was. But I suppose I'd read about it in a poem that I liked, so I decided to put it into my own. But you see, I was merely imitating *other people's* poetry. I had to learn how to write poems about the things that were part of *my* life." Mrs. Macdonald tapped her chest hard, making a hollow sound.

"So I can understand why Wendy might want to keep her poems to herself for the time being," she went on. "I hid my first poems. I wrote them on old letter bills discarded at the post office. One of my problems, you see, was finding paper. We used slates, of course, in school, and often I no sooner had a pretty poem written on my slate than I had to erase it for an arithmetic problem."

Then she smiled broadly and slapped her hand down on the desk. "I remember the day I decided to try a poem out on someone. My grandmother had an acquaintance to tea one day. This woman was a singer, and I asked her rather shyly whether she knew a song called 'Evening Dreams.' Of course I knew she didn't, because there was no such song. It was the name of a poem that I had written. But I wanted a chance to recite it and get a reaction from her. She shook her head and said, 'No, I don't know that song, but if you recite a few lines of the verse, perhaps I'll remember the tune.' So I recited the whole poem, and she said sweetly that she didn't know it at all, but the words were very pretty. Well, I was in ecstasy! Someone actually liked my poem!"

Laura laughed. "Did she ever find out that it was your poem?"

Mrs. Macdonald shook her head. "I don't think I ever saw the woman again, and I suppose she never found out that she was my first audience. But I owed her a great deal for her compliment. Perhaps Wendy will try the same trick out on you some day."

"Was that when you started sending your poems and stories away to magazines?"

"Yes, perhaps it was soon after that episode. I eventually won a contest or two and had poems published as a result."

"What did you win in the contests?"

"Just the recognition. Knowing that my poetry was appreciated by experts and seeing my poems in newspapers, one in faraway Montreal—that was enough for me. I was on top of the world."

"Was that when you knew you really were a writer?"

"By the time I was a teenager, I was serious about my writing career. And by the time I was teaching school I was sending poems and stories to magazines all over North America." She picked up the sheaf of papers again and leafed through them, reading passages to herself from time to time and chuckling.

"I started feeling really successful around the time I entered a contest that was sponsored by the Halifax *Evening Mail*. The question we had to write on was, 'Who has more patience, men or women?' I wrote a long poem in which I argued—of course—that women have more patience. And what do you think happened?"

"You won the contest!"

"That's right. And five dollars! Right after that, I had one story after another accepted by American magazines. One publication, I remember, paid me twelve dollars for a poem."

"Were you going to university in Halifax at that time? My grandfather met you there and you told him you had to fight to get an education."

Mrs. Macdonald hunched her shoulders, closed her eyes and let out a long sigh. Then she sat close to Laura looking her straight in the eye. Her face was serious. "Don't ever let anyone deprive you of an education. It is every person's right." She sat back in her chair and continued. "Of course, nowadays it's different for girls. They take it for granted that they have as much right to an education as boys do. But in my day, it was expected that a woman would simply get married and be looked after by her husband, and that was the end of it. It didn't occur to most people that a woman might like to earn her own living and be independent, or that a woman might like to have knowledge beyond running a household."

"But you *did* get an education."

"Oh, yes I did. My grandparents didn't want me to go to Prince of Wales College for my teaching license, but in the end I talked them into it. And for that year that I spent at university in Halifax, I had to argue bitterly with them."

"But you won the argument."

"Yes, eventually. It was my grandmother who relented, and she even helped me pay for my tuition. My grandfather remained bitterly opposed. He thought that the world had come to an end because his granddaughter wanted a university education. And I remember a neighbor asking me why I wanted to be educated. She wondered if I wanted to become a preacher!"

"A preacher?!"

"Well, this was the 1890s. Girls *might* do some training to become a nurse or a teacher—but to study at the university? Girls from Cavendish?!" She threw back her head in mock horror. "Times have changed, thank heavens."

They sat for a moment in silence, looking out the rain-spattered window. Then Mrs. Macdonald heaved herself up from the chair. "Look how we've been avoiding the work of sorting through my books!"

Laura remained seated, ignoring her remark. "When did you start writing books?" she asked, looking up at her.

Mrs. Macdonald sat down again and threw up her hands. "I give up. You've got me reminiscing so much I can't get down to the business at hand."

Laura grinned and said nothing. She felt a cramp in her leg and shifted her position on the footstool.

"It began with *Anne of Green Gables*, of course," said Mrs. Macdonald.

"Did you just sit down one day and say, 'I'm going to write *Anne of Green Gables*?'

"Not at all. It began as a story like all the rest, a story about a girl. But the more I wrote, the more I realized that I had a lot to say about this particular girl—more than I could put into a story. I remember clearly the day when I thought to myself, 'This story is turning into a book!' It was a warm spring day, and through the open window I could hear the birds chirping down in the apple orchard. And there was another thing about this little girl...." She sat up straight and spread her hands on her knees.

"Most of the publications I wrote for demanded that my stories have a moral in them, and...."

"A moral?" asked Laura.

"Yes. That is, the stories had to teach a lesson, something that would inspire the young readers. The stories couldn't just be rollicking good yarns. They had to be about good little girls, or about wicked little girls who became good after something dreadful happened to them. And I wanted to write about a *normal* girl—someone who got into scrapes and who was sometimes naughty as well as good. I wanted to bring characters to life and tell a good tale. Sometimes a good tale doesn't have to have a 'moral' to it."

"So Anne was the kind of girl *you* wanted her to be?"

"That's right. I was tired of having to create characters that showed children how to behave."

"Where did Anne's story begin, in your head, I mean?"

"Well, Anne's story began with an idea that I jotted down one day in the little notebook I was telling you about. An elderly couple that I knew about wanted to get a boy from an orphanage to work on their farm, and the orphanage sent a girl instead. I suppose when I jotted it down, I thought, 'Hmm, what an interesting mistake!'" She stopped talking for a moment and watched as the rain dashed furiously against the window. "A good soaking. That's what the earth needs."

"Was it fun not having to make her into a goody-goody?"

"Fun?" She furrowed her brow and rested her elbow on the desk. "Much as I love creating characters, I have never thought of it as 'fun'. But yes, I truly loved writing *Anne*. But getting the book published was another story. I sent it off to three publishers, and it came back, one, two, three. *Rejections!* Of course, when you're a writer you get used to rejection slips, but I must say after all the time and work I put into it, I did feel let down. So I put the thick package of typewritten pages away in a hat box and forgot about it."

"What did you do then? Did you go back to writing about boring little good girls?" Laura put her hand over her mouth. "Oh, I shouldn't have..." she began.

"Why not? It's true. They *did* feel dreary after Anne. I suppose I was so disheartened that I had little choice." She straightened again and smiled at Laura. "But as you know, the story of getting *Anne of Green Gables* published has a happy ending."

"What happened?"

"Three years later I came across the manuscript of the book one day when I was housecleaning, and I started reading it again. I thought to myself, 'This isn't half bad,' and I decided to send it away one more time. So I sent it to the publisher L.C. Page in Boston, and lo and behold, it was accepted!"

"Were you excited?"

"'Excited' is too tame a word. I'll never forget that first time, when I received the book from the publisher in the mail and looked at the cover—'*Anne of Green Gables* by L.M. Montgomery.' Do you know how books smell when they're new, and how crisp the pages are?"

Laura nodded.

"Well, I kept putting my face in it, smelling it and feeling the pages. I ran my hand over the cover with that lovely picture— not *my* imagined picture of Anne, but handsome all the same—

and then finally I opened it to the dedication page. 'To the memory of my mother and father.' I thought to myself how proud they would have been of me. And my goodness, the exhilaration of it!"

"Was your grandmother proud of you?"

Mrs. Macdonald's face clouded over. "I wish I could say she was. But she never appreciated my writing. 'I don't know why you're doing that scribbling,' she'd say. My success with *Anne* meant nothing to her." She adjusted her glasses and sat tall in the chair. "But *Anne* has meant a lot to many, many readers, and I'm grateful for that. Still...."

"Did your grandmother ever read it?"

"I don't think so. But enough of that. Why dwell on it?" She stood up. "You must be getting stiff sitting cramped up like that. Come downstairs. Let's see what's happened with the forsythia."

She led the way downstairs to the dining room. In the centre of the table, the bouquet of forsythia buds had burst into flower.

"I'm sure Anne would have had some splendiferous thing to say about that forsythia," said Mrs. Macdonald. "But Anne is long behind me. All I can think of to say is, 'Don't these signs of spring make you glad to be alive?'"

Chapter Eleven

"Lemonade makes me think of the twenty-fourth of May and the first of July," said Laura as they sipped from the glasses Mrs. Macdonald had brought back to her writing room. They were once again seated, Laura on the needlepoint footstool and Mrs. Macdonald at the desk.

"Why is that? Because they're holidays and the weather is fine and you're outdoors having good times?" asked Mrs. Macdonald.

Laura nodded.

"How does Rocky Falls celebrate Queen Victoria's birthday and Dominion Day?" asked Mrs. Macdonald.

"Both times the whole town has a day of sports. They set up a booth in the park and sell hot dogs and lemonade and ice cream, and we have three-legged races and other games, and there's a baseball tournament. It's fun because all my friends are there together."

"It always seems to me that spring is truly here when the twenty-fourth of May rolls around. Then by the time Dominion Day is upon us, it's truly summer. With those holidays, we seem to be celebrating the passing of one season into another."

She took a sip of lemonade. Her mouth puckered slightly. "What would winter be like if there were no spring to look forward to?"

"Boring," said Laura.

Mrs. Macdonald laughed. "I think perhaps 'boring' is your favourite word." She drained her glass and stood up. "No more excuses for me. I'm finally getting to these books. Shall we work on them together?"

"While we're working, Mrs. Macdonald, will you tell me about some of your other books?"

"There's not much to say about them. Once one has been written, I go on to the next one. All that's left is for them to be published and read." She stood beside Laura looking down at the shelves of books with the name of the author, L.M. Montgomery, on the spines. She bent over and pulled one off the shelf. "Here it is, the one I was telling you about awhile ago. The first edition of *Anne of Green Gables*." She brushed a thick coat of dust from the top of the book and blew off the rest. "It's been many years since I have removed it from the shelf," she laughed. "My housecleaning skills must have slipped in the last few years." She ran her hand over the cover in the way she had described earlier, and then gently opened the book.

"This book changed my whole life," she said in a quiet voice. Her delicate hands turned the pages slowly. Here and there she stopped, scanning a page. "People have asked me over and over again whether Anne was someone I knew. That is a lovely compliment, because it means that I was truly able to bring her to life. But of course she was not a real girl, nor was she like anyone I knew. She was simply a product of my own imagination."

"Why did she have red hair? Did you make her that way on purpose?"

"That's very hard to say. I just don't know the answer. The imagination works in strange and complex ways. I've always liked red hair. My wonderful chum from long ago, Will Pritchard, had red hair, as did some others that I've been fond of. Some incidents in the book were taken from my life, but then I changed them according to the way it seemed best for the story. The episode of the puffed sleeves, for example. Do you remember how Anne desperately wanted a dress with puffed sleeves and Marilla said puffed sleeves were just vain nonsense and wouldn't let her have one? Do you remember that?"

"Uh-huh." Laura nodded. In pictures she'd seen of women in old-fashioned dresses, the huge gathered sleeves that mushroomed out from their shoulders looked ugly. She remembered wondering why Anne bothered making such a fuss over such a silly thing.

"They were all the rage at one time. A girl considered herself the height of fashion if she wore a dress with puffed sleeves. Well, I didn't care so much about puffed sleeves, but, as I told you a few days ago, I *did* care about bangs. I felt my grandmother was unjust in not allowing me the simple pleasure of wearing my hair the way I wanted. So, when I came to write about Anne, I remembered that feeling I'd had years before and I made it Anne's feeling as well. By that time, bangs were no longer the fashion, and so I changed the particular item to suit the changed times. My bangs became Anne's puffed sleeves. Nowadays it might be...."

"Doing up your hair in pincurls," said Laura. "Or wearing nylon stockings. Or...."

"Yes, I'll bet there are any number of things you could substitute for Anne's puffed sleeves. But the important thing is that you can *sympathize* with her. You can understand her feelings."

"Oh, yes," said Laura with enthusiasm. "I sure can!"

"You might want to give this advice to your friend Wendy. Tell her that if she can create characters that readers can sympathize with, even if they don't particularly like these characters—if readers feel they *know* these characters, a writer has created a successful story. Wendy must have done that, however," she added, "if she won a contest for the whole county."

As Mrs. Macdonald was speaking, Laura had squatted down and was pulling some of L.M. Montgomery's books from the shelves. Mrs. Macdonald set down *Anne of Green Gables* and took two others from Laura.

"*Rilla of Ingleside, The Golden Road*," said Laura, reading the titles.

Mrs. Macdonald held one in each hand, turning them over, looking at the back covers, then at the pictures on the front.

"You know, Laura," she said at length, "I'm not proud of much that I've written. Oh, *Anne* was good, and so was *The Story Girl*. The *Emily* books are dear to my heart. But I'm not sure about the others...."

"But why?" asked Laura. "I can hardly wait to read them all. And I hope you'll write more. Will you?"

Mrs. Macdonald shook her head slowly. "I don't think so. I think my writing days may be over." She held up *Rilla of Ingleside*. "I wrote this book during the last war. I was so dreadfully crushed by the horror of it that the only thing I could do was to pour my feelings into my writing." She looked closely at the cover for a few moments. "You haven't read this one yet, have you?"

"No," said Laura. "What's it about?"

"It's about Anne's daughter. In this book, Anne is middle-aged and her children are young men and women. Rilla is the youngest. She's named after Marilla, the woman who adopted Anne."

"And is Rilla the main character?"

"Yes, she is. The story of the war is seen through her eyes. Her two older brothers—Anne's two oldest children—enlist and go over to Europe to fight. The townsfolk are in frenzy of worry because, of course, there's someone from nearly every family who has gone off to the war. Several times a week news comes to one family or another that one of their sons has been killed. And one day, of course, that news comes to Anne's family...." She stopped and gave a wan smile. "These are only made-up characters, but when I create them, they become alive for me. Anyway, they learn that Walter, the brother Rilla is closest to, has been killed in battle. I think that's the hardest thing I've ever written. I cried as I was writing that passage. If I write another book, it may have to be about the war we're going through now. Anne's grandsons, perhaps—no, I don't think I could do it."

"Why didn't you just change the story so that Walter didn't have to die? Maybe he could have just been missing, and then...."

"And then have a happy-ever-after ending? No, of course not. I could never have done that."

"Why?"

"Such is the imagination, I'm afraid."

Laura wasn't sure what Mrs. Macdonald was talking about. "Why? Why does he have to die?" she insisted. "And why did Matthew have to die in *Anne of Green Gables*?"

"Well, death is a part of life. If I didn't make some of my characters die, it wouldn't be the way real life is. By the way," she said, still looking at the two books in her hand, "how are you getting on with *The Story Girl*?"

"I finished it yesterday. It was so good I didn't want it to end. I wish I'd been there in the story with them all."

"Ah, you've paid me a wonderful compliment by saying that. It means that I've brought my characters to life for you."

"I liked Cecily the best."

"Let me tell you about Cecily...." She stopped and held up *The Golden Road*. "No, on second thought I won't. You'll have to read this to find out. *The Golden Road* continues the story of all those young people."

Laura felt cold. "She doesn't die, does she? I don't want to read it if she does."

"My dear, that is not only a narrow-minded approach to literature, it is an ostrich-in-the-sand approach to life! We are fortunate that there is also beauty and friendship in life." She put the two books down. "No more distracting discussion now, my dear Laura. Let's get back to work. I'm going to get a step ladder so that we can get to the top shelves." She disappeared and returned a moment later carrying a step ladder and a cloth duster. "I'm going to get you up on this ladder and ask you to give me the names of those books on the top shelves, and while you're at it, you can give them a good dusting."

Laura positioned the step ladder and climbed up, the duster in her hand. Mrs. Macdonald pulled a brown ledger book from a drawer. For a long time the silence in the room was broken only by Laura's voice calling out the titles and the *whish* of the duster as she rubbed the tops of the books. The pelting of the rain still sounded against the window.

The two of them jumped when a knock came at the door of the writing room and Mary appeared, whispering that lunch was ready.

Mrs. Macdonald looked at Laura. "You will stay for lunch?" She pushed back a loose strand of hair and fastened it underneath her hairnet.

Laura nodded. "Yes, thank you."

✧

When they returned upstairs after lunch, Laura heard Mr. Macdonald muttering and groaning from behind one of the closed doors.

"Go inside. I'll be with you in a minute, my dear," Mrs. Macdonald said with a tremor in her voice. Laura noticed that her head was shaking and her face pale.

In the writing room, Laura picked up *The Golden Road* from where Mrs. Macdonald had laid it down, settled herself in the author's chair and began reading. She immediately joined the same cast of characters she thought had ended with *The Story Girl*, on the King farm in Prince Edward Island. On the second page appeared hints of Cecily's fate—the gentle girl's cheeks shone with an unnatural rosy colour and she seemed out of breath. Laura then riffled through the rest of the book. As each page appeared, winter turned to spring, and there were weddings and amusing escapades, and the Story Girl's announcement that she was to go with her father to Paris and Bev and Felix's news that they were to return to Toronto. Finally came the Story Girl's fortune-telling session with each of them. When Cecily begged for *her* fortune, the Story Girl balked.

Mrs. Macdonald returned to the writing room still pale. Her head shook a bit, but her hands were still and she appeared calm.

"Cecily doesn't die in this book," said Laura, holding up *The Golden Road*. "But she's sick, and you know that she isn't going to live much longer."

"I don't think I had the heart to kill her off just like that," Mrs. Macdonald answered, taking the book from Laura's hands and leafing through it, her white hands caressing the pages. "It would have been too difficult. The best thing I could do was to simply allude to her death." She put the book down again and surveyed the book shelves.

"Back to work," she said. "We make a good team." She put down the books and moved across the room to another book-case. "Now these," she said, indicating a row of poetry books. "It's hard to keep my books apart from Ewan's. I'd like to sort out my poetry books, and then some of those history books that I've read over and over. Then finally there are the novels. Dickens, the Brontës, Jane Austin...." She pulled down one of the books she had been pointing at. Laura couldn't see the title, but she saw that it was well-worn. Some of the pages seemed to have come loose. Mrs. Macdonald's body suddenly seemed to crumple, and she grabbed the chair and slumped down in it, still clutching the book. She remained sitting and staring into space.

"Mrs. Macdonald," Laura began, moving beside her.

Hesitating a bit, she put her hand on Mrs. Macdonald's shoulder. It felt bony and hard. She didn't know what to say.

"Do you know what dissatisfies me about my books, Laura?" Mrs. Macdonald said finally.

Before Laura had a chance to respond, she went on. "All these years I've never developed another book that was better than *Anne of Green Gables*. Oh, perhaps *The Story Girl*, but nothing beyond that. Nothing like this." She raised the book she was holding, and Laura now saw the title in faint letters. It was called *Wuthering Heights*.

"That is what has always eluded me—the chance, or perhaps the ability, to write a truly *good* novel," she went on. There are times whem I am proud of the pleasure my books have given young girls like yourself. Then there are other times.... But my mind was so taken up with Ewan's condition and my sons' problems and my church work that I wasn't able to write anything but "potboilers", as I call them—but I mustn't blame anyone. I could have dug deeper with my writing spade."

Her voice drifted away, and her head leaned back. "But I didn't," she finished as her eyes closed. It seemed to Laura that she might be falling asleep. Her face looked drained. She put her hand over Laura's, which still rested on her shoulder. It felt cold to the touch. "I think I can do no more today, Laura," she said with a small smile.

"Mrs. Macdonald," Laura said, grappling for words, "*I* think your books are *wonderful*."

Mrs. Macdonald held Laura's hand tightly. "Thank you, dear Laura," she whispered.

✧

A few moments later, they stood in the tiny vestibule as Laura put on her jacket. Mrs. Macdonald held the door open, her hand twisting and turning the doorknob in spasmodic movements.

"Maybe it'll be sunny tomorrow and we can work in the garden again," said Laura.

Mrs. Macdonald shook her head slowly. "The forecast is for continued rain. It looks like we're having a brief return to cool weather before we move headlong into spring. Spring will come, however, and when it does, it will be...." she swallowed hard and her head began to shake.

"Infinitely sweeter than we imagined it," said Laura.

Mrs. Macdonald nodded. "I couldn't have said it better myself," she answered.

"You *did* say it yourself," said Laura, "at the end of *Story Girl!*"

Mrs. Macdonald blew her a kiss and closed the door.

Outside, Laura shivered against the damp cold. She stood in front of the house for a moment, not wanting to return right away to Grandpa's house. She kicked at a stone, and sat on the step, staring into space, ignoring the rain. She looked around at the work they had done along the side of the house and as her eyes roamed back and forth across the lawn, she noticed a purple dot. Kneeling in the damp grass, she saw that it was a tiny violet. Looking up, she saw another, and then another, a blanket of violets on the lawn.

As she walked down the flagstone path, she saw that across the street, Sam had roused himself from in front of Grandpa's house and was trotting toward the gate to meet her.

Chapter Twelve

Downstairs the next morning, Grandpa sat alone in the breakfast nook, toast crumbs on his plate and a half-drunk cup of coffee in front of him. He was reading a letter. On the table lay the envelope, and inside, blue airmail paper was visible.

"Ah, my Laura," he said, glancing up as Laura came into the kitchen. "I'm reading a letter from your mother. It's just come with the morning mail." He looked back at the letter. "The fine weather we had earlier this week has continued up in Rocky Falls and the flood warning has been called off. They've had hardly any of our rain, it seems. School opens again Monday. She wants you back home on Sunday if we can get a seat for you on the train."

Laura sat down opposite him. She looked around at the velvet blossoms of African violets surrounding her, then looked out the window. Birds were flying back and forth from the feeder in the back yard. She remembered her homesickness and loneliness the first day she arrived, just over a week ago, and now she wasn't sure she wanted to go. She turned and ran to the wall calendar. "Today is Friday. That means I have only two more days here, today and tomorrow. Can't I stay a bit longer, Grandpa? Mrs. Macdonald needs my help."

Grandpa shook his head. "Maud would be the first to say that you need your education more than she needs your help."

"I know," said Laura. "Still I wish...." She looked around the kitchen, suddenly realizing that Bobbie wasn't there. "Where's Bobbie?" she asked.

"Bobbie telephoned me last night to say she's joining up."

"Joining up?" Laura was puzzled.

"One of the women's corps. I wouldn't be surprised if the next time we see her she'll be in uniform. And as for me—I'll have to be looking for a new housekeeper. I don't know if I'll be able to find one, with all the women working now that so many of the men are overseas. I may have to do my own cooking and cleaning, Laura. Imagine a man my age learning to cook!"

"I'll cook for you!" said Laura eagerly, for the moment forgetting that she didn't really know how to cook herself.

Grandpa laughed and was about to retort when Laura interrupted. "Did Andy leave her?" she blurted out.

Grandpa nodded. "She said there was a letter from him when she got home yesterday. He had already left—took the train to Halifax and expected to be sent overseas any day. He said in the letter that he wanted to call their engagement off for the time being."

"Was she unhappy?"

"Well, yes, I suppose so, but this way she can begin a new life for herself." He picked up the envelope that was sitting on the table. He handed it to Laura. "How could I have forgotten this? Your mother included your father's latest letter. Here, read it. But get yourself some breakfast first."

With her mouth full of toast, Laura unfolded the blue airmail letter. It felt like tissue paper. The writing, in blue ink, was barely discernable in places. He had moved out of London, her father wrote, but before he left he had seen the King and Queen driving by. And the two princesses!

"I'm settled here now, in the Canadian General Hospital in Surrey, doing surgery," he wrote. "I'm safely in the countryside, and I expect they'll keep me here until the end of the war. So the only action I'll be seeing will be the work I have to do on the wounded boys they bring back to England. Just know that I'm fine, except that every time I see a little girl, my heart aches. But it won't be long now, let's hope, and keep those home fires burning...."

Laura stopped reading and looked up. "Dad's not in danger. He's working in the hospital and he's safe."

Her grandfather smiled. "A relief to us all," he said. Then he got up to leave. "Another reason you'll have to go home— there's no one here to look after you now that Bobbie's gone. I'll be back later, of course, and tomorrow we'll go to the station for your train ticket. We'll have to cancel the movie and our visit to the library. In the meantime, for today, I hope you won't be too lonely. Maybe...."

"I'll be fine, Grandpa. I'll go over to Mrs. Macdonald's."

After Grandpa had left, Laura busied herself washing up the few breakfast dishes. Then she swept the kitchen floor and filled Sam's water dish as she'd seen Bobbie do. She'd never noticed the clock in the hall before, but now the only sound in the house was its loud ticking. Outside, a horse clip-clopped by, and she opened the front door to find that a bottle of milk had been left. She stooped to pick it up and looked across the street. Perhaps

Mrs. Macdonald would be ready for her to come over now.

She stood in the drizzle outside the house. Sam had bounded outside when she had first opened the door, and Laura bent over to stroke him.

"Stay here, Sam," she whispered, and before the dog had a chance to trot alongside her, she was out the gate and crossing the road. At the Macdonalds' front door she paused, then rapped. There was no sound but the rain, soft now, falling into the evestrough overhead.

She rapped again and waited. She heard a shuffle inside, and then the door opened a crack. Mary's face appeared.

"Not now, Laura, not now," Mary whispered in a tight voice.

"I came to help again," said Laura. "It'll have to be my last day. I'm going to the train station tomorrow to get my ticket home. School is opening again on Monday."

Mary shook her head slowly.

"But please let me at least say good-bye to Mrs. Macdonald!" Laura cried.

"I'll have to say good-bye for you," said Mary, her lips moving like a fish mouth as she formed the words through the crack in the door. "She's very low. And he's gone crazy."

She shut the door and Laura stood alone in the rain.

Back inside Grandpa's house, she wandered from floor to floor. The basement seemed like a cavern. The white washing machine stood in a corner covered with a cloth. The rinsing pans were hung neatly on the wall. Upstairs, the bedrooms were in perfect order. Laura remembered that Grandpa said how lucky he was to have such a good housekeeper. On the mat by the kitchen door, Sam sighed and grunted and got up once in awhile to slurp some water from his dish. Otherwise there was no sound except the ticking of the hall clock. The living room was a like a tomb. Laura looked in Grandpa's bookcase for something to read, but the books looked heavy and boring. Grandpa didn't even have any magazines.

A pack of cards that she and Grandpa had used in the evenings for rummy sat on an end table. She took it out and played game after game of solitaire. At some point she fell asleep on the sofa. She was still asleep when Grandpa returned later in the afternoon.

✧

"Grandpa, there's something I forgot to tell you," said Laura as she skipped down the stairs the next morning. "Mrs. Macdonald told me about her books, like you said she probably would...." She stopped suddenly.

Grandpa was waiting for her at the bottom of the stairs. He looked up, his face drained. His hair seemed long and unkempt, and his moustache, for the first time, seemed rather scruffy.

"Laura," he began, and then a sob escaped from his lips. He pointed toward the door. "Laura, Maud's gone," he whispered.

Laura ran to the door and opened it. For the first time in several days, the sun shone. The branches of the oak trees across the street were swollen with green shoots. In the driveway across the street stood a long black car. Other cars lined the road. She turned back toward her grandfather.

He nodded. "She died last night," he whispered. He stood bent, like an old man, the skin of his face almost transparent, the veins pulsing his temples.

Laura opened her mouth, but nothing came out. She stood

that way, breathing in and out through her mouth until it became so dry she had to run her tongue over her lips. Her grandfather stumbled into the living room and sat down on the sofa, still bent over, and clenched and unclenched his hands. "Why does it always hit me this hard?" he asked, staring down. "It's like a blow to the stomach."

Laura sat on the edge of the chair opposite him. She didn't know what to say.

"It always happens this way, whenever I hear of someone from the old crowd down home passing away." He shook his head, still looking down at his hands. "I see it happen every day in the hospital, so you'd think I'd be used to it. But I can never get used to the thought that the friends of my youth are no longer with us. And when I think of Maud Montgomery, I think of a girl flying down the road with grey eyes and a long mane of hair, a girl sitting in the woods surrounded by other young folk, holding them in the palm of her hand as she spun her tales. I never think of Maud the way we saw her on Sunday—frail and unwell."

"Was she—what happened to her?" Laura felt numb.

"Oh, I'm sure we'll hear eventually. Right now...." He shook his head.

Laura sat down on the edge of the sofa. She couldn't picture Mrs. Macdonald—dead. Not the woman who had bent over the plants with her gardening gloves a few days ago, who threw back her head and laughed at some of Laura's questions, who blew her a happy kiss. How could she have died?

"There was always something romantic about Maud," Grandpa continued. "Always something sprightly, as if she would get up and dance a jig with you for any reason whatever."

His head bobbed up and down, and Laura noticed that his hair was white rather than grey on top and that through his thinning strands his pink skull shone. "Of course, I never asked her to dance, though I wanted to. She was a popular girl, and I was an awkward lad."

He sat back in his chair and squared his shoulders somewhat. "You know, though, there was something else about Maud. There was always a bit of unhappiness about her. As if underneath all the high-jinks and the story-telling she wasn't as jolly as she let on. It was as if she longed for something."

Laura stared into space.

"She had a tendency to look inside herself," Grandpa continued. "That would be the poet and the writer in her, I suppose. When you write something, you have to look inside yourself for inspiration. But I wonder if Maud sometimes brooded a bit too much. You'd notice how she'd go off by herself and wander in the woods or sit by the lake or watch the waves on the seashore. It isn't good for the health to brood too much. Still...."

He sat up straight, his voice gaining strength. "Still, when you think of it, a young girl living in a tiny village on the edge of Canada, with no help from anyone—it makes you proud to think of what she accomplished!"

Laura wasn't listening. She continued sitting, stunned, her hands clasped in her lap. She looked over at the smiling picture of herself and her mother on the mantelpiece. How could she go home now? All she wanted to do was dash across the street, knock on the door and hear Mary tell her that Mrs. Macdonald was in the back yard pruning the bushes, waiting for her help.

✧

She didn't remember how long she sat in the living room staring around her, at Grandpa's bookcase, at the mantelpiece, at Grandpa's bowed head, and at the buds forming on the trees outside.

The next thing she remembered was riding on the streetcar later with Grandpa on the way to Union Station to buy a train ticket. It seemed like she was entering another world again when they entered the huge, bustling building.

This time, here and there among the servicemen, she noticed women in uniform that she hadn't seen before, wearing jackets with brass buttons, and shirts and ties like men. Some of them wore jaunty caps and some were bare-headed. Some were dressed as nurses, in white uniforms and navy blue cloaks. She thought of Bobbie and wondered, with an empty feeling, if she would see her again. And then she thought of Mrs. Macdonald. How could everybody be going about their business here when Mrs. Macdonald had just died? Didn't they care?

Returning along Bloor Street, Grandpa said suddenly, "Let's get off the streetcar here."

"Why, Grandpa?" asked Laura when they were standing on the sidewalk. "This isn't our stop."

"It just occurred to me that you might like to go the library, even if you can't take a book out. It will be a visit in memory of Maud." Grandpa was smiling again. He still looked sad, but his face had regained its colour, and he didn't look like the old man who had greeted her this morning.

The sun was shining high in the sky as Laura and Grandpa walked toward the library. People were out on their lawns, clearing their verandahs, bending over plants, raking their lawns. In one garden a cluster of daffodils was ready to burst into bloom.

"Look, Grandpa," she said, grabbing his arm and pointing to the daffodils. "Won't Mrs...." she swallowed, remembering. "Wouldn't Mrs. Macdonald be excited to see the flowers coming up?"

"That's a result of all the rain we've just had," said Grandpa. They approached a school, and he stopped, looking up at it. "Here we are," he said.

"Where's the library?" asked Laura.

"Why here, in the school," said Grandpa.

"In the school? Isn't it in a house all its own? In Rocky Falls the library is in a white house."

"Oh, I'm sure Swansea will eventually have its own library too. In the meantime, it's housed here in the public school."

They entered the school through an entranceway beneath a bell tower.

"I've never seen a real school bell before," said Laura. "Does it ring when school is ready to start?"

"I suppose these school bells are soon to be a thing of the past," said Grandpa. "When we went to school, Maud and I and the rest of those long-ago chums, the school bell was one of the most familiar sounds around. Now they'll soon be ringing electric bells to call the children to their classes, I suppose."

Inside, there was a hush. Book shelves lined the wide hallways of the school, broken only by the doorways leading to classrooms. At the end of the hallway sat the librarian behind a brown desk. Grandpa greeted her.

"It's a sad day for us today," the librarian said. "I don't know if you've heard the news."

Grandpa nodded. "Yes," he said.

"She was a valuable member of our library board. We were so fortunate that she lived in our little part of the world, and that, famous as she was, she devoted so much of her time to our modest library."

"I didn't know she had anything to do with this library," whispered Laura to Grandpa.

"I daresay Maud devoted her time to a lot of things," he whispered back. "She was a generous woman."

"How was she generous?"

"She tried in her own way to be kind. She lent money to all kinds of people. And it was well known that she answered every single letter that was written to her by the fans of her books. Letters mostly from girls like yourself, I imagine. They'll treasure those letters now that she's gone."

"I wish I'd gotten a letter from her," said Laura.

"Oh, my dear, you've received much more," said Grandpa, and then he put his finger to his lips to indicate silence.

Laura walked the length of the hallway, looking over the book shelves, and, as she passed by the classrooms, she peeked inside. They were all similar to her classroom back in Rocky Falls. She was surprised that as she looked inside them she felt a surge of satisfaction at the thought that she was heading home. She realized she missed school.

"Books for girls your age are along this side," said the librarian coming up to her. Laura looked over the shelves of Nancy Drew books, and her glance briefly alighted on a set of nurse books. Then she kept moving slowly along until she reached what she was looking for. There they were, book after book by L.M. Montgomery.

"If you've read *Anne of Green Gables*," the librarian said, "may I suggest you try...."

"But I don't live here! And I'm going home tomorrow. I wouldn't have time to read it."

"Oh, that's too bad. She's actually autographed a number of her books on our shelves. Perhaps the next time you visit."

Laura and Grandpa walked home along the lake. As they headed up the hill, Laura looked over at the wide curve of the Humber River that Mrs. Macdonald had spoken of so fondly.

Approaching Grandpa's house, Laura refused to look at the house across the street. "I don't want to see it anymore," she said to him.

At the sound of the gate opening, Sam rose from the mat in front of the door and stood to greet them, his big ears flapping.

"What's this?" said Grandpa, reaching up to the mailbox outside the front door. Propped up inside the box was a brown package. A message was scrawled in pencil on one side of it. Grandpa frowned as he tried to make out the words. "'Mrs.— Macdonald—left this—for Laura'," he read. "Oh, so this is for you." He handed the package to Laura.

She opened the package and saw that it was a book. The title was *Emily of New Moon*. The author was L.M. Montgomery. On the cover a girl stood facing the sea. Her hair was done up in bangs and braids. Laura opened the book slowly. On the inside page was inscribed, in shaky handwriting, "*To Laura, my friend and kindred spirit. Thank you for bringing spring back into my life.*" It was signed, "*L.M. Montgomery Macdonald.*" Laura held the book tightly as Grandpa opened the door.

Then she leaned against the doorframe and sobbed, her shoulders shaking.

✧

The next day, Laura stroked Sam's ears as she and Grandpa waited for the taxi.

"Good-bye, Sam," she said. "I'll be back to visit."

"Here it is!" said Grandpa, picking up Laura's suitcase. Laura grabbed her knapsack. Sam, whimpering, stood gazing at them as they headed for the taxi which had just pulled up to the gate. Laura didn't look back at him, nor did she look across the street at the Macdonalds' house.

"She blew me a kiss the last time I saw her," she said to Grandpa as they settled themselves in the back seat. "That's how I'm going to remember her. She looked almost happy when she did that."

A short while later, Laura stood with Grandpa among a milling crowd in front of the train. She watched the steam spew back from the engine as they waited for the train doors to open and the stairs to unfold for the passengers to climb aboard.

Laura looked up at her grandfather. His cap sat forward on his head. He still seemed bent and fragile. For a second she wanted to say, "Let's go home, Grandpa." She'd stay and look after him and keep house for him. Somehow, she'd learn how to cook. Then she pictured Mrs. Macdonald as she sat at her desk in her writing room looking out the window at the pine trees on the ravine. "Don't let anyone deprive you of an education," she remembered her saying.

Just then she heard another familiar voice. "Laura! Dr. Campbell!"

Laura turned. A tide of rough serge uniforms brushed past her face on all sides. Then, as if a pathway had opened, Bobbie rushed toward them, her face flushed. She wore a brown uniform and on her feet, instead of her usual pumps, were brown oxfords. She stooped to kiss Laura, and Laura could smell no perfume this time, but only the clean smell of soap and new clothes. Her fingernails were clear and unpolished.

"Bobbie!" Laura cried, and then the crowds pushed against her and she was swept up and onto the train. She turned briefly to see Bobbie waving, her curls dancing against the crispness of her uniform.

On the train, Laura's grandfather saved her a seat by the window and as the other passengers jostled to get their belongings settled, he lifted her suitcase onto the overhead rack. Then he gave her a reassuring smile and touched her shoulder.

"Before you know it, it'll be summer and I'll be up to see you and your mother. If I can manage it, I might even bring Sam."

They hugged for a long time and then he was gone, and Laura was alone. She stared out the window for what seemed like hours at the steel rafters and lines of tracks. Then the train began to move. Laura opened her knapsack and pulled out *Emily of New Moon*. She put her knapsack down at her feet, and as the train gathered speed, she opened the book and began to read.